The Book of David

The Book of David

Anonymous

Simon Pulse

New York   London   Toronto   Sydney   New Delhi

SIMON PULSE

An imprint of Simon & Schuster Children's Publishing Division
1230 Avenue of the Americas, New York, NY 10020
This Simon Pulse edition June 2014
Text copyright © 2014 by Simon & Schuster, Inc.
Cover photograph copyright © 2014 by Getty Images/ZAM-Photography
All rights reserved, including the right of reproduction in whole or in part in any form.
SIMON PULSE and colophon are registered trademarks of Simon & Schuster, Inc.
For information about special discounts for bulk purchases,
please contact Simon & Schuster Special Sales at 1-866-506-1949 or
business@simonandschuster.com.
The Simon & Schuster Speakers Bureau can bring authors to your live event.
For more information or to book an event contact the Simon & Schuster Speakers
Bureau at 1-866-248-3049 or visit our website at www.simonspeakers.com.
Book design by Karina Granda
The text of this book was set in Adobe Caslon Pro.
Manufactured in the United States of America
10 9 8 7 6 5 4 3 2 1
Library of Congress Control Number 2014930951
ISBN 978-1-4424-8986-8 (hc)
ISBN 978-1-4424-8985-1 (pbk)
ISBN 978-1-4424-8987-5 (eBook)

The Book of David

Monday, August 27

First day of school, first period. Mrs. Harrison is making us all keep a journal for English Literature. We don't have to turn it in. We just have to write in it for the first ten minutes of class on Mondays, Wednesdays, and Fridays—or the last ten minutes, whichever she decides that day. It's weird to write with a pen in class. Usually I take notes on my laptop. My hand is already cramping up. The good news is that my handwriting is so atrocious, I'll be the only person who can read it, so I don't have to worry about anyone else deciphering this.

When Mrs. Harrison announced the journals, Tyler groaned like Coach was forcing him to run line drills. Mrs. Harrison told Tyler there's something physiological that happens when you write with a pen or pencil on actual paper. He said, "Yeah, my brain shuts down because it's so bored." She just rolled her eyes and told him to "hush." Tyler said he didn't have anything to write about, and she told him the point is to not stop, to keep your hand moving across the page even if you think you don't have anything to say. Then she held up a legal pad and a pen at the front of the class and pretended to write across it while she said the words out loud as an example:

"I have nothing to write about in my English class, but my crazy-ass teacher is making me keep a journal anyway. I hate her so much, I have smoke coming out of my ears, which I wish was

1

bong I can't tell anyone I own because my
...iggs and I'm a starter on the high school football
...get caught I will lose my scholarship to one of the
...colleges that send scouts to Hillside High to watch
me p... ...us, I will not get to start in the game on Friday night,
and my pretty cheerleader girlfriend will think I am a loser."

The whole class cracked up—even Tyler. Mrs. Harrison is
our favorite teacher. She's tough, but she says stuff like "crazy-
ass" and makes jokes about pot, which she can get away with
because she's such a good teacher and because her husband is
the music pastor at the big Baptist church most of us attend.
She's up front every Sunday, singing in the choir.

Actually, nobody knows who the starting lineup is for sure
yet. List will be up this afternoon before we hit the locker
room. Coach has been playing both me and Tyler at QB this
summer. I'm glad two-a-day practices are over, but I'm nervous
as hell about him posting the lineup. Tyler's my best friend and
has been since seventh grade. I know how much this means to
him. We've been pushing each other since we were in junior
high—lifting, running, making sure our grades are decent—and
it all comes down to this: Only one of us can be starting QB our
senior year.

Tyler's got seven pounds on me, but I've got two inches on
him. He can rush like a locomotive (takes three linemen to drag

him down), but I can leap and scramble. Under pressure, he likes to tuck the ball and plow down the field like a tank. I fall back and look for the pass. It's all up to Coach now.

Mrs. Harrison is right about the scouts, too. They've been hanging around practice all summer. Tyler told me last week that he's ready to give a verbal commitment to Arkansas. I've been holding out for Oklahoma.

I just heard this new kid sitting next to me flip to his third page. He's writing like his arm is robotic. His hair is wet and he's wearing a T-shirt that says THE SMITHS. I wonder if that's his last name.

Dang. Mrs. Harrison just told us to wrap it up. Can't believe it's been ten minutes already.

Wednesday, August 29

Everybody moaned when Mrs. Harrison told us to take out our journals today. She rolled her eyes and wrote MY BIGGEST SECRET on the whiteboard in blue marker. She said that was our topic for today's journal entry and reminded us that no one would be reading these journals, so we could be completely honest.

Yeah. Right.

Crap. My pen is running out of ink.

I was just digging through my backpack, looking for another pen while everybody else was writing. The new kid across the aisle is wearing a T-shirt that says THE WHO today. ("The Who"? "The Smiths"? Who are the Smiths is my question.) Anyway, he must've seen me because I felt a tap on my shoulder, and when I looked up, he was holding out the pen I'm writing with right this second. Write this second. (HA! Get it? *Write* this second?) I kill me.

I whispered, "Thanks," and he smiled at me, but not just with his mouth. He smiled with his eyes, too, and that's when I noticed how crazy this kid's eyes are. They are blue, but not like a standard factory preset sort of blue—this kid has eyes that are a special feature sort of blue. He probably thinks I'm a total freak show, because I said, "Thanks," and then just stared at him. I realized after a second that my own smile had fallen off my face and I was totally locked with this dude's eyeballs, and my heart was speeding up and I felt like I couldn't swallow and my stomach dropped even further than it had when Mrs. Harrison wrote today's journal topic on the whiteboard.

The weird thing was, this kid didn't look away. He just held my gaze, and his crazy blue eyes narrowed one-one-hundredth of an inch, like he was asking me a silent question. Then he brushed a stray piece of wet hair off his forehead and winked at me.

I almost jumped out of my skin when he did that. I dropped the pen he gave me on the floor and reached down to grab it so fast, I banged my head on my desk. Mrs. Harrison looked up and asked if everything was all right, and I nodded and mumbled "yes" and "sorry" at the same time, so it sort of came out as "yaarry," and Tyler snorted a laugh from his desk behind mine. I felt my cheeks turn bright red, and I'm afraid to look anywhere except this page in my notebook because it feels like the entire class is staring at me. Everybody must've seen him wink at me, and his smirk, and I'm such a freaking dumbass for not having an extra pen in my backpack. Now I bet every single person in the room has their mouths hanging open, wondering what just happened. I can't stand it. I have to know if everybody is looking at me.

Weird. I just glanced around superfast and nobody is looking at me. Nobody suspects anything.

Except the new kid.

When I glanced up just now, I saw his wet, wavy hair. It's sort of long on top and buzzed close on the sides. He's bent over his desk, writing so fast, it looks like his pen might spark against the paper and set fire to the whole building.

But he's smiling.

Not big.

Just a little curl at the edge of his lips, peeking out of the scruff on his face. He's got a five-o'clock shadow, like one of those dudes on cable playing the bad-boy cop turned spy for hire who wears his mirrored aviator sunglasses all the time— even at Miami dance clubs at two in the morning. And how does he manage to have stubble? I only have to shave once a week. Even when I forget, it doesn't grow in even like his does. My beard is sort of blotchy and—

Damn.

He caught me looking at him again. Eyes on the page. Keep your hand moving. Act like you have nothing to hide. Act like nothing happened. Even though it did happen. Twice. He caught you looking at him *twice.* You freaking *moron.* If Tyler saw that wink, or looks at that new kid and sees his smirk, he's gonna razz you for weeks. Just write. Write. Don't look. Don't think. Just keep the pen going. See? You can do this. You don't have to think about the new kid and his eyes and his stubble and his smirk and his weird-ass T-shirt collection and why in the hell his hair is always wet, and *jeez*, I'm doing it again.

Okay. New paragraph. Tyler is sitting right behind you. Football. Write about football. List went up Monday. Tyler is starting QB this year. I'm bummed but happy for Tyler. I'm starting Friday as a running back. Coach said he thinks that's where I'll get the most attention from the scouts. I wanted to tell him I'd get the most attention from the scouts if I were starting QB. I wanted to punch my locker and yell, but that's not how I roll. I'm the cool, calm, collected one. I don't break my hand. I don't raise my voice. I'm the yin to Tyler's yang. I'm chill under stress, which ironically, makes me a better QB than

Tyler. I know how to scramble while I find the perfect pass or the perfect path. I can move my feet without taking my eyes off Press or Chris while they sprint to get open. I can pass a hundred yards more than Tyler will ever be able to rush in any game, but Coach loves Ty. He loves watching Tyler scramble through the crunch. He's not into precision. He's into blood and guts.

Christ. If Tyler ever saw this, he'd freaking flip. He's my best friend. I should be cool with this. Monica tried to cheer me up. She pulled me out to the parking lot after the list went up and kissed me really long and slow with lots of tongue. She said it was to make me feel better, but it just reminded me that she's captain of the cheerleading squad and she's supposed to be going out with the quarterback. Isn't that the way it should work? Now I'm dreading having to hand this pen back to the new kid. I'm dreading having to even talk to him at the end of class. I'm supposed to be the cool, calm, collected QB. But now I'm just another meathead running back.

WHY DO YOU CARE WHAT THE FREAKING NEW KID THINKS?

YOU DON'T.

Mrs. Harrison just said to wrap it up. You don't owe anybody an explanation. Running backs get great scholarship offers. And who gives a crap what anybody thinks? Especially wet head in "The Who" shirt. I mean, what is going on with him and his smirk? What was it that passed between us when he winked at me? I have no idea what just happened.

But I have a feeling he does.

He knows exactly what just happened.

He knows my biggest secret.

Friday, August 31

Tonight is the home opener. Can't think about anything else. Just want to get out there and be playing. Nothing is worse than the anticipation. Or better. It makes me feel like I'm coming out of my skin. My hands are sweating just thinking about the smell of the grass, the crunch of the helmets and pads, and the roar of the crowd. And Monica screaming over it all to B-E AGGRESSIVE.

Tyler and I have been drilling hard all week in practice, and Coach has made us run a fake snap over and over. Ty drops back to pass, and I dart out of the line and run behind him. He throws his arm forward like he's passing but drops the ball back to me. Hopefully, this will draw off the defensive line and allow me to shoot out the side and run for my freaking life down the side of the field. The first time we ran the play, Coach had told only the two of us and it worked like a charm. By the time our defensive line had figured out Tyler didn't have the ball, I was in the end zone. I could hear Tyler cussing a blue streak at

Brandon Sears. He's this monster black dude who transferred in from Jefferson last year. Six feet five inches and roughly the size of an apartment complex. We call him Sears Tower. He just about crushed Tyler's spinal column, but we ran the play two other times, and it was only the third time that they were looking for it. Still made a five-yard gain before I got flattened. Just glad it wasn't Brandon. I'd like to live to see my eighteenth birthday—which is tomorrow, actually. I'll be able to vote this year. And be drafted. But not drink. Legally, anyway. Weird that I'll be old enough to die for my country but not to buy beer. That regulation is screwed up. If I can be taught to fly a fighter jet, I should be trusted with a six-pack of Corona.

Not that I'll have any shortage of beer tomorrow night. Monica's parents are out of town, and she's throwing this monster surprise party for me at her place tomorrow night. I'm not supposed to know about it, but like we always say around here, the two fastest forms of communication are text message and Tyler-phone. Somehow he's sweet-talked an ex of his older brother's into getting him two kegs. She and her friends are supposed to bring them over to Monica's after the game. Why college girls want to hang out at a high school kegger is beyond me.

The hard part is getting through today without tipping off Monica. She's wearing her cheerleading uniform, and she was actually skipping down the hall next to me on the way to first period just now. She's got trig first period. Monica has more brains than the rest of the girls on the varsity squad combined, but I'm pretty good at keeping a poker face. She'll never figure out that I already know about the party.

Besides my unsurprising surprise birthday party, she's also really jazzed about the pep rally this afternoon. We'll all get out of seventh period early, and by that time, Mr. Chadwick will have posted the cast list for the school musical, which is the third reason Monica can't stand still today. She was telling me all about the auditions earlier this week. I'll just say it: I do not understand musicals. I get what they are, but musicals represent zero form of any reality I've ever seen. I mean, I guess there are weirdos who do flash mobs, but that's just public dancing. It's not like people walk down the street and suddenly burst into a song about their day and dancing strangers join them in four-part harmony.

Monica says this year's show is called *The Music Man*. It's about a librarian who falls in love with a con artist. She's auditioned for the role of the librarian named Marian. I can only assume there are lots of songs that rhyme the word "librarian" with the name "Marian." I'm already bored just thinking about it. Not to mention that this is precisely what I mean about musicals not making any sense. Monica is *way* hotter than any librarian *I've* ever seen.

Saturday, September 1

I can't believe I'm doing this. Yes, it is Saturday. Yes, I am slightly hungover. Yes, it is my birthday. And yet here I am, writing in the journal I'm supposed to keep during English class. With a pen. I don't really know why except that something feels right about putting this all down on paper. A lot happened last night, and I just think I'll feel better if I write it down. Also, I want to remember it. I'm afraid if I don't get it all down right now, I won't remember how I feel about what happened last night. Or maybe I'm afraid that I just don't know how I feel about it at all. I think I'm all mixed up about it, and maybe if I put it down on paper, I will figure out how I feel about all of it.

Jeez. If Tyler saw me doing this he would roll his eyes and say, "That's so gay, dude," which brings me to Tyler, one of the reasons I have to write about yesterday.

We were losing by ten at the half last night. Jefferson was creaming us, which was stupid because we're a better team. Tyler was not having a good night. I could tell he was all amped up before the game. I mean, he's usually rocking and rolling around school all day before a game. He doesn't even have to drink one of those crazy energy drinks—he's just got that much adrenaline when we've got a game. Anyway, he told me before the game that the Arkansas scout was meeting him afterward, and I guessed that meant he was going to tell them he was going to accept their scholarship offer. He gave me a weird look and said, "Maybe." Then he told me that Oklahoma was sending a scout to the game tonight, too. I asked him what he was saying, and he looked at me and grinned. "Wouldn't it be awesome if we played on the same team in college, too?"

It's weird, because if he'd asked me that at any other moment in the last six months, I'd have said, "Hell, yeah!" But for some reason, a bomb went off in my chest, and I got real quiet. I couldn't make my mouth work 'cause I was afraid of what might come out of it. I felt like I was gonna yell at him. It took everything I had not to yell: You dumbass. Oklahoma is *my* school. That's *my* offer.

But why would I be mad? I mean, Tyler's my best friend. Shouldn't I want to get to play on the same team with him in college? I didn't have time to think about it. I just nodded and muttered something like, "Oh, cool," and then we hit the locker room and Tyler was doing that thing he does: tearing around, pounding on lockers and helmets and snapping the jockstraps of lowerclassmen and leading the whole team in this chant that involves a lot of roaring (because we're the Lions) and how we're the kings of the jungle.

I couldn't even join in. I just tossed my bag on the bench at my locker and pulled off my shirt while I kicked off my shoes. I was shucking off my jeans when it hit me: I was jealous.

Which is so stupid.

Tyler and I have been neck and neck in the national quarterback rankings since sophomore year. We've both risen through the ranks within five positions on the list. We started out in the seventies, and now he's fourteen and I'm seventeen. It's not like he's got anything on me. I know this in my head, but somehow I didn't know it in my gut. I was just pissed off that he was starting quarterback. While I watched him standing on a bench in his boxers roaring like an imbecile at the top of his lungs, I felt like he'd taken it from me somehow.

I stared too long, 'cause all of a sudden he stopped and turned and looked at me. He realized I wasn't yelling. That's the thing—Tyler might *act* like an idiot, but he's not. I saw his eyes narrow, and that damn smirk spread across his face, and he yelled my last name. Every head turned to look at me. "You staring at my abs again?" He rubbed his hands down his stomach, thrust his crotch out in my direction, and grabbed his junk. "This'll make you ROAR, baby."

I should say right now that this is normal for Tyler. He makes these jokes about everybody. It's one of the things that cracks me up about him. It's one of the reasons that we're best friends, but somehow this was different. There was a glint in his eye, and I was mad anyway, and then I made the fatal mistake and blushed.

I've dealt with my secret for long enough to know what I have to do to stay under the radar. I know where to keep my eyes in the shower. I've been practicing not getting a boner in the shower since I was in seventh-grade PE. My voice isn't too high. I carry my books against my hips and not my chest. I know how to talk about girls. I know how to talk *to* girls. I know how to get the captain of the cheerleading squad to be my girlfriend for two years. I've got this down to a freaking science. The one thing I can't figure out is how to keep from blushing. I've got blond hair and blue eyes, and even though I can get tan and don't burn in the summer, I blush like a little girl. It starts on my ears and spreads down the back of my neck, then shoots around my entire face.

Tyler knows this, and when he decides it's my turn on the chopping block, there's nothing I can do about it. I covered pretty fast, but Tyler saw the blush. And even though I covered, even though I did what I always do and take the douche thing he's doing and give it right back to him, even though I jumped up there in my underwear and roared and yelled about shooting his lion with "these guns" while I flexed my biceps, Tyler knew he'd gotten to me. He saw the blush, and he knew I was pissed. He knew what it was about, too, 'cause as soon as everybody went back to the general business of padding up and getting dressed, he came over to his locker right next to mine and said,

"Dude. Chill out. I thought you'd be happy about Oklahoma. Not trying to steal your thunder."

The truth is, Tyler has been like a brother to me. I just don't know if I want to have to keep dealing with this weird competition with him for the next four years.

I just looked at that last sentence and realized that I *do* know. I *don't* want to continue this weird competition with Tyler.

Of course, I didn't know how to tell him that at the time. How do you find the words to tell your best friend why you don't want to play college ball with him? That you don't want to have to put up with his bullshit antics anymore?

If he knew who I really was, would he still hurl all those jokes my way? Does he actually already know somehow? Is that why he's making these cracks? Is that why they feel like grenades aimed right at my head?

I hate myself for being a coward. For not being able to say these things to his face or to ask him these questions. If we're really like brothers, shouldn't I be able to?

But there he was, doing that thing he does, coming back and giving me as close to an apology as I ever get: "Chill out, dude."

I hated myself for blushing. I hated myself for not being just a normal guy who could take anything he dished out without getting all freaking sensitive about it. None of the other guys had caught on, but Ty sure did. He knows me better than anybody else—as well as I'll let him know me. That's the double-edged sword of having a best friend.

That's also why I can't stop thinking about what happened next. Namely, that we went out and started losing to Jefferson. Bad. We won the coin toss; then three plays after kickoff, Tyler threw an interception. It wasn't really his fault. Corey Tracker, one of our wide receivers, had his hand on the ball and just tripped. Tracker is a sophomore. He's fast as a mofo, but he gets excited and forgets to do things like check his shoelaces. He went down hard, but not before batting the ball right into the hands of a Jefferson safety, who ran like a goddamn greyhound all the way down the line and right into the end zone. Nothing went right for us after that, and just before halftime, Jefferson scored a field goal.

Coach lit into us like Brad Pitt in *Fight Club*. I decided I'd rather be crushed at the bottom of a tackle than come back into the locker room without a touchdown in the second half. Tyler must've had the same thought, because as soon as Coach broke his clipboard and told us to get the hell back out on the field and play the game like we'd been playing all summer in practice, Ty bumped my knee with his and whispered, "First play is the Snap." I said no way. Coach had told us both to hold on to that one. He wanted to practice it a few more times before we used it in a game. Tyler just looked at me and said, "Jesus. Grow a pair."

So I did.

He called the play in huddle. We broke. Ball snapped. I circled, and Tyler pulled off the fake perfectly. He didn't even look. He dropped back to pass at precisely the right moment and just trusted me to be there when he dropped the ball backward and threw his arm forward. I was in the end zone before Jefferson even realized he hadn't thrown a pass. The crowd went berserk. Tracker was right behind me and came running at me. He grabbed my helmet, and it was while we were roaring at each other through our face masks that the crowd went silent.

I turned around and saw the huddle in the middle of the field and I knew exactly what had happened. Tyler had gotten nailed after the fake.

This weird fear that had been hiding out behind my sternum since Ty told me the OU scout was gonna be there tonight exploded up toward my throat and down toward my stomach. Then I was running back down the field. The silence of the crowd was eerie. It all happened so fast that by the time I got to where he was, Tyler was being loaded onto a stretcher. I knew it was bad. They don't bring out a stretcher unless they think it's an injury that has to be stabilized. If it were a sprain, or a hard hit, they'd have walked him off.

Coach turned around and looked right at me and shook his head once. "You're up." I nodded, but I was staring after Tyler, and Coach got in my face. "Hey. He'll be fine. I need your head right here in this game." I said, "Yes, sir." He hit my butt and said, "Hey, do that touchdown thing again, will ya?"

I did.

Twice.

I was a machine. Whatever weird fog had settled over us in the first half lifted completely. Those Jefferson monsters were hitting hard, but I kept dropping back and nailing Tracker and our other running back, Mike Watters, and if neither of them was open, this fast freshman kid we'd been calling Flash all summer would just magically appear and we'd pick up twenty yards, then thirty yards, then *blam*: end zone. I hardly heard the crowd. I couldn't even hear Monica cheering. I could only feel the guys shoulder to shoulder in the huddle, the words of the next play on my tongue, the rough snap into my hands, the ball spinning off my fingers. I passed for almost as many yards in the second half of last night's game as I'd passed total in every practice this summer.

When it was over, we were up by ten, and as the clock ran out on Jefferson's last play, Coach and I watched from the sidelines for a second as the crowd spilled out of the stands and went running toward a pileup in the middle of the field.

A split second before Tracker and Sears Tower hoisted me up on their shoulders, Coach looked me right in the eye and said two words I'd never heard him say in the three years I'd been playing for him:

"Thank you."

I saw the water cooler get emptied over Coach's head right as Monica and a bunch of the cheerleaders and their friends descended on me. Somehow my parents found me at the exact same moment, and it was like a massive group hug and celebration dance, with people shouting and screaming and crying and generally acting like idiots.

Finally the crowd started to die down. Monica was talking one hundred miles per minute, and she had that new kid from English with her. I almost didn't recognize him 'cause his hair wasn't wet. He was smiling and wearing a T-shirt that said THE CURE. She kept calling him Jon and talking about how they met, but I didn't really catch the story. I didn't know she knew him, and I was really surprised to see him there. He walked up and stuck out his hand and said, "Congrats, man. Nice game."

It was the weirdest freaking thing. Like, all this pandemonium is going on all around us, and he isn't yelling or anything. He just smiles and says, "Nice game," sort of quietly. And even with all the noise and the crush and the craziness . . . I heard him.

I reached out and shook his hand, and it was like everything else just faded down to a dull roar—like in a movie where everything goes slow motion all around the main character, and all he can see is the big explosion that's taking place right in front of him. Only this time it wasn't an explosion. It was just me staring into Jonathan's eyes. He held my gaze as I shook his hand, and for a split second it was like there was nothing else in the world—just me, and him, and our . . .

Connection.

My dad had been tailgating before the game with Tyler's dad. They always broke the rules and smuggled beers in from the parking lot, and he was still pretty drunk. He was almost crying with joy, and he stumbled into Jonathan and knocked us both sideways, hooting and hollering and belching the smell of Miller Genuine Draft all over the place. Jonathan laughed, and I snapped back to the present. Monica was giving me instructions to hurry up and get cleaned up because the party at her house was already starting and it was going to be "off the hook." I saw Jonathan turning to leave and heard myself say, "Wait!"

Monica thought I was talking to her and stopped too, but I was looking at Jonathan. Monica said, "We have to hurry. They're meeting us with the . . . supplies."

"No—" I didn't know how to ask. "Is he . . . ?"

Monica got this weird look on her face and followed my gaze to Jonathan.

"Uh, yeah. Jon is coming."

Jon. She calls him Jon.

"I'll be there." He smiled at me again, and I felt myself blushing, but I didn't care. Monica ran back and pecked me on the cheek, pulling my face down to look at her.

"Hurry!" she commanded. "The whole party is for you, birthday boy. At midnight you're eighteen!"

This all happened in the general craziness while Dad was hugging me and kept shouting, "That's my boy! That's my boy!" over and over again. As Monica and Jon headed across the field, Mom told me I did a good job and kissed me on the cheek, then dragged Dad back to the car. He turned around and shouted, "Stay out as late as you want. You earned it." He almost took down this blond woman wearing a business suit and high heels who was standing over by the bleachers by the entrance to the locker rooms.

She looked like a lawyer you'd see on one of those TV shows about cops where there's a different killer every week. She was tapping away at a smartphone, and when Dad almost sent her into the stands, she didn't yell at him or anything. Just dropped her phone into her bag, smiled at them, and righted herself. Then she turned and raised her hand like she was hailing a taxi and called my name.

I was sort of shocked. I'd never seen her before in my life, and I was a little annoyed because I was hoping the scout from Oklahoma had hung around, but I didn't seen anybody who looked like a scout, so I was getting bummed out pretty fast. What if he hadn't made the game? What if he'd left after Tyler got hurt and didn't see me pull this one outta the fire? What if he was waiting for me on the other side of the locker rooms by the doors that led out to the parking lot? I had to get over there to check.

I smiled back at the woman as she ran a hand through her long blond hair and then extended it to me. She had dark red nails, and as I shook her hand, I was vaguely aware that Tyler would have called this woman "a total MILF" and my dad would have referred to her as "a stone-cold fox."

She introduced herself as Alicia Stevenson.

"Good game tonight, sir."

"Thanks," I said. I had to keep walking. Couldn't get stuck chatting up somebody's . . . mom? Aunt? She didn't look old enough to have a kid in high school. . . .

"Do you have a second to chat about college?" she asked.

"College?" I was confused.

"Won't keep you," she promised. "That cheerleader and her friend seemed to be planning a big party that requires your presence." She pressed a business card into my hand. It was thick, heavy stock, and I could feel the print raised against my fingertips. When I glanced down at it, I saw an Oklahoma logo and it hit me:

"Wait, you're—you're the . . . ?"

"Scout. Yep, that's me. Call me on Sunday, when you have a minute. I want to talk to you about the possibility of coming to play for us at Oklahoma. I think there's a place for you with the Sooners."

"Wow—sorry, I didn't . . . I mean, I wasn't expecting—"

She cocked her head and raised an eyebrow. "A woman? Don't worry. No one ever is. And I wasn't expecting you to pass like a pro out there tonight. Came to see Tyler, but we've already got a great running game, and—well, let's just say I'm convinced this worked out for the best."

She turned and walked on her toes across the sod toward the concrete so her stilettos wouldn't sink into the grass. When she reached the sidewalk that led to the parking lot, she turned and waved. "Talk to you Sunday!"

I watched her heels *click-click-click* toward a sleek gray car. She opened the door, flipped her mane over her shoulder, then melted into the seat. The last thing I saw was her long leg disappear into the driver's side door.

It's weird when something happens that you've been hoping would happen for a really long time. I guess I always thought it would make me jump up and down and scream like an idiot, or lose my freaking mind, but it was strange. That's not how it went. Instead this feeling of certainty washed over me and made me feel like anything was possible. It wasn't a big crazy rush. It just felt . . . *right*.

When I walked into the locker room, I felt like I was floating. I stood under the shower with all the guys whooping and hollering and running around snapping each other with towels, and all I could think was, *I did it. I'm gonna play ball at Oklahoma.* I felt calm and sure of myself. I felt like this was supposed to happen, that this is where all the hard work of the last few years was supposed to lead—to being ready to step up in this moment. This conversation with Alicia Stevenson was the next logical step after working as hard as I could to be the best I could possibly be. This was all that dedication—all the sweat and swollen knees and jammed fingers—finally paying off.

I turned off the shower and grabbed my towel. There were so many high fives and slaps on the ass by the time I got back to my locker, it's a wonder I'm not bruised. I just smiled and felt so certain—so sure of myself. For the first time in my life, I felt like . . . a man. I knew what I wanted and where I was going, and finally I knew the road to take to get there.

As I was getting dressed, Coach came by and asked, "Did she find you?"

I just looked up at him and smiled. I didn't have to say a

word. Coach nodded back. "Attaboy. Go have fun tonight."

I asked him if Tyler was okay. His face told me the whole story. "He's at Baptist. I just talked to his dad a minute ago. They're doing a CAT scan. Looks like it might be his ACL." Coach shook his head, then shot me a look. "Don't you worry about any of that tonight. Go celebrate. You deserve it."

I did want to celebrate, but I felt bummed about Tyler not being there. I headed out to my truck, and instead of driving toward Monica's place, I turned and drove to Baptist Hospital. I parked and walked in through the emergency room doors. I saw Erin sitting there with her mom. Her legs were long and bare under her cheerleading skirt, and she was wearing a big sweatshirt and a Windbreaker. It was freezing in there, and it took her a second to recognize me. She smiled when she did, but I could tell she'd been crying. There were tracks of mascara and glittered eye shadow shining on her cheeks. She came over and hugged me.

"Heard you did good," Tyler's dad said.

"No fun winning with Tyler hurt." I'm not sure why I said that. It just seemed like the right thing to say, and I could feel Tyler's dad soften a little when I said it. "How is he?"

Tyler's dad shrugged. "Screwed."

"Can I see him?"

"Nah—they've got him all trussed up back there. Doing

MRIs and crap. Taking a million dollars' worth of pictures to tell us what we already know. He's out for the season."

"Maybe it's not as bad as we think." I felt helpless. It was a mistake to come here. Tyler and I were competing for the same spot on the field, the same scholarship money, the same headlines in the local sports section, the same attention from the same scouts. Alicia Stevenson had basically confirmed it. There was no way that Tyler getting hurt wasn't good for my football career. This was a fact that hung in the air over all of us like the smell of gasoline when you accidentally drip it on your shoe. It fills the car, and there's no way to ignore it.

Erin held up her phone. "Sounds like you did great tonight. Everybody's still texting and tweeting about it."

Tyler's dad huffed through his nose, then tried to cover it up with a quick smile. "Yeah, champ. Thought you'd be out celebrating."

There was nothing I could say to make this better. "Well, Tyler's my best friend. I wanted to at least come see how he was doing. I'm worried."

At that moment, Tyler's mom pushed through the big double doors from the ER into the waiting room. Her face lit up when she saw me. She hurried over and hugged me.

"It will mean so much to Ty that you came to check on him," she said. "He was so happy you mopped the field with those guys."

I smiled sheepishly. I felt guilty about doing a good job now.

"What's the word?" Tyler's dad was all business.

"Won't know for sure until the morning, but it looks like they can fix it with some surgery."

Tyler's dad huffed again. His mom patted his shoulder and then turned to me. "Don't you worry about Ty. He'll be running around causing trouble in no time."

"Not on the field." His dad's eyes were watering. "He's done with football in high school. He'll be lucky to keep the offers he's got."

Tyler's mom shot his dad a look, then smiled at me. "You kids should get going," she said. "I think there must be a celebration going on somewhere, and Tyler's sleeping here tonight. Can you give Erin a ride?"

"Sure," I said. "I'm really . . . sorry. About all this. Will you tell him I came by?"

Tyler's mom hugged me again. "Of course, sweetheart. This was not your fault. You have nothing to feel sorry about."

I knew in my head she was right, but the ache in the pit of my stomach got a little worse every time I remembered Tyler's dad snorting and shaking his head and saying, *He's done with football in high school.*

My stomach was still in knots when Erin and I parked by the curb at Monica's place, and it didn't get any better when

Flash handed me a red plastic cup full of beer. Corey Tracker and Brandon Sears were trying to keep the college girls who had brought the keg from leaving—flirting their asses off. The girls were bummed because they'd been lured to the party with the promise of Tyler, but every time Tracker filled their cups, they giggled a little louder as the foam splashed out and ran over their fingers and seemed to be warming to the idea of doing without Tyler for the night.

Monica spotted me and came running over dragging Jonathan and her friend Amy from the cheerleading squad. "There you are. Jeez. What took you so long?"

"He was waiting for his curling iron to warm up." Tracker was laughing so hard at his own joke, it was easy to reach over and flip his beer all over his shirt. He yelled in mock protest, then poured what was left in the cup over his own head and melted into the college girls who insisted they "get him out of these wet clothes" while pulling his T-shirt off.

"Stopped by the hospital," I explained. "Brought Erin."

"Oooooh, heeeeey, Erin." Amy was the cheerleader most likely to be drunk first. "How's Tyyyyyyyyler?"

Erin put her arm around Amy to keep her upright. "He's alive, but he's going to have to have surgery to fix his knee."

Jonathan let out a low whistle. "So he's out for good."

"Says who?" Sears was really tall and really slow. It worked on the field, but in conversation it could be a chore. "Anybody know this guy?"

Monica threw an arm around Jonathan's shoulders. "This is Jon, everybody. He just transferred here from a school in Chicago, and he's going to be the lead in *The Music Man*."

Jon opened his mouth to say something, then closed it again. This was not the introduction he had hoped for. Even Tracker and the college girls were suddenly silent, staring. This truck was headed over the cliff.

"That's awesome."

Sears, Flash, and Tracker all turned to look at me, and I realized I was the one who had blurted out those words. I blushed like a mofo, but it was dark except for the bonfire, which had just sparked to a full blaze a couple hundred feet away. Lots of shadows. I plowed ahead. "I forgot the auditions were today. Did you find out the cast already?"

"No," said Monica with her imperial smile. "I just know talent when I see it."

"I'm on the swim team, too . . . ?" Jon offered this fact sheepishly—as a question: *Will this help balance that I'm the drama geek?*

"So that's why your hair is wet in English every day."

"Yup." He smiled at me, relieved—a silent thank-you in his single syllable.

Tracker was too drunk to care about anything except handing out beer, it seemed, the way of freshmen at their first big party after their first big win their first year on varsity.

"Hey, Music Man," he brayed, thrusting a foaming red cup at Jon. "I'm the beer man. Drink up."

Jon sidestepped the slosh with a lighting-quick reflex and laughed. "No, thanks, Beer Man. If I'm gonna drink, I prefer the good stuff." He smiled and passed the red cup to Amy, who'd been reaching for it anyway. She giggled a thank-you in Jon's general direction as he pulled a bottle of Maker's Mark out of the messenger bag he had slung over his shoulder.

"Aw'ight, fancy-pants!" Sears howled. "Now you're singing a tune I know, Mr. Music Man."

Half a bottle of Maker's later, the knots in my stomach had dispersed like the crowd. After Jon won over Sears, Tracker, Flash, and the college girls with the power of Kentucky straight bourbon, they headed for the hot tub. Too many roasted marshmallows at the bonfire made Amy start to barf (typical), and Monica and Erin helped her up the long expanse of lawn toward the switchback stairs that led up several terraces from the river to the pool.

"Back in a second," Monica chirped at us. "You boys get acquainted while I get little Pukey-Pukes-a-Lot here up to my bedroom." Erin giggled and tried to hold Amy's hair to one side as the three of them did a weird six-legged race toward the house.

"Does she always drink this much?" Jon stared after them.

"Amy?" I smiled. "Of course. Her dad's a preacher."

Jon nodded with a knowing smile. "There does seem to be a direct correlation between the drunkenness of a cheerleader and her proximity to the laity."

I stared at him. "Huh?"

Jon laughed, and something about it sounded like the notes of a song I remembered from a long time ago. Maybe it was the Maker's or maybe he really is the music man. Whatever the reason, my heart was racing and I laughed with him.

"Sorry," he said. "When I get tipsy, I use my English vocabulary words."

We were sitting on a log by the remains of the big fire. The last couple kissing on the other side finally stood up and stumbled deeper into the woods to make poor choices in private, and I felt Jon bump my knee with his. Something about the touch of his leg against mine sent a spark straight through me like the loud *crackle-pop* from the fire in front of us, which sent a shower of embers into the Arkansas night over our heads.

When I turned, Jon was smiling and holding the bottle my way. I grabbed it and took a swig. The thick, sweet liquid burned all the way down, and the warmth in my throat matched the heat of the place on my leg where Jon's knee had bumped mine.

I passed the bottle back, and my hand brushed Jon's as he took it and swung it up to his lips. Why did I notice every tiny contact I had with him? It was like my skin was on fire, and he was covered in pins and needles. I took a deep breath, and even though it was a humid August night, a chill swept over me. I felt the hair on my arms stand up with goose bumps.

"So . . . happy birthday."

"What . . . ? Oh, yeah!" I said with a laugh.

"Did you forget?" he asked. "Wasn't this whole festival of sin in your honor?"

"I guess—kinda, yeah."

"So, you're officially a man. How's it feel?"

I shrugged. "I dunno. Kinda . . . tipsy."

Jon smiled and handed me the bottle. "Finish it off, birthday boy."

"You got it, Music Man."

He groaned. "Goddammit. That's gonna stick, isn't it?"

I gulped down the last of the bourbon and tossed the bottle in a high, long arc into the river. It landed with a *klerplop* in the middle. "Shoulda led with the swim team thing."

"It's fine," he said. "I *do* like music."

Jon stood up next to me and stretched. His shoulders were broad from all that swimming, and the bottom of his T-shirt hiked up above the belt loops on his skinny jeans. Even in the dim light from the dying fire I could see chiseled abs disappearing into the waistband of his underwear. I thought about Tyler earlier in the locker room and felt my face go hot. I tried to look away, but Jon glanced down just as I did. Caught twice in twenty-four hours? I was getting sloppy.

Jon smiled and cocked an eyebrow. I knew he was about to make some crack, but my mind was blank.

To my surprise, he said nothing, which made my cheeks burn even hotter and forced me to try to say something—anything—to explain myself.

"I—uh—I was . . . looking . . . at your T-shirt!" It came out too fast and too loud and too much like I was . . . well . . . an idiot. I'm blushing again just writing it down.

Jon was staring at me, searching my face for a hidden answer I wasn't sure was there. He slowly pulled the hem of his T-shirt out and down a few inches from where it hung and glanced at it.

"This ol' thing?" He said it in a slow, lilting Southern drawl like he was in a movie. If he thought it was weird I was staring at his stomach, he didn't let on.

"What are pixies?" I asked, pointing to the words on his shirt.

He glanced down at the writing, then smirked at me. "A pixie is a fairy or a sprite," he said. "Especially a mischievous one."

33

Something about the way he said it made it sound like he was quoting from the dictionary, and I snorted through my nose, which made him laugh, too. He sat back down on the log next to me.

I was wiping tears out of my eyes from laughing so hard. "So . . . wait . . ." I gasped. "Why do you have a T-shirt promoting mischievous fairies?"

"Dude. It's a band."

"Really?" I asked. "Never heard of 'em."

"I'm not surprised. They don't get a lot of play on Redneck-Country-104."

I shot him a look. "Redneck country, huh?"

He met my gaze and held it. "You're one of those 'Achy Breaky Heart' types, aren't you?"

Something about the way he said "Achy Breaky Heart" made my irritation about being called a redneck melt away. Or maybe it was his smirk. I started laughing again. "Achy Breaky Heart? Like . . . Miley Cyrus's dad? C'mon, man. He sang that song before I was born."

"Yeah, but admit it." He was totally going for it now. "You're a big ol' country lover at heart."

"Well . . . yeah." I smiled. "Maybe I've never heard The Pixies, but do you know any George Strait?"

Jon stared at me. "Strait?"

"Yeah. What's wrong with 'Strait'?"

He smiled in this way that made me unsure what we were talking about. He raised his eyebrows and gave me this big innocent grin. "Nothing," he said. "Nothing at all."

We were silent for a couple seconds. I was so buzzed that all I could do was stare at the glowing embers.

Jon broke the silence. "I wanna hear some."

"Some what?"

"Some George Strait."

I looked at him. I could see his face in the glow of the embers from the bonfire, and his eyes glinted, full and serious. No smirk.

"Really?"

"Yeah," he said. "Send me a playlist. Or burn me a CD. Or whatever. I'll make you one of The Pixies."

"Okay." I smiled at him. "Where'd you move from again?"

"Chicago."

I groaned. "Yankee."

He laughed. "Yep."

"What made ya'll come South?" I asked.

He shrugged. "Dad got a job."

Jon didn't seem to want to talk about it. We sat there for a while on the log by the fire, listening to the music from the party up at the house and the sounds of the river. I felt warm, and alive, and ready to bust—like there was this energy surging through me. It crossed my mind that maybe we should go back up to the house and find Monica and Amy. How long had we been down here, just the two of us? But the truth was, I liked hanging out with Jon. I didn't want the girls around. My legs were itching like I needed to run. I imagined Jon and me jumping up and whooping and racing down to the edge of the river, then running along it for miles until we were in the middle of nowhere.

"I don't really think you're a redneck," he said.

I laughed. "I may be a *big* redneck. I drive a truck. I listen to country. I have no idea what your T-shirts mean, Yankee."

"They're all bands."

"All of 'em?" I asked. "The Who? The Smiths . . . ?"

He looked surprised. "Somebody's been paying attention."

My stomach dropped like I was on the kamikaze waterslide at Wild River Country. "I just . . . I mean . . . You were . . ." I was stuttering all over the place. Suddenly he reached out and grabbed my knee.

"It's cool." His hand on my knee made me jump like he'd dropped an ice cube down my shirt. My heart was racing again. His fingers left my jeans, but I could still feel the heat of where he had touched me, the weight of his palm burning through the denim. "Didn't think you'd end up trading shots with the drama geek tonight, did you?" His smirk was back.

I laughed. How did he do that? One second he had me jumpy as a cat in a room full of rocking chairs and the next second, he cracked me up.

"What were you doing at the game tonight, anyway?" I asked. "The theater kids don't usually show up."

"Journalism assignment. I'm supposed to post about the game on the school blog Monday."

"Journalism?"

"Yeah, they asked for a volunteer to write up the home opener."

"And you volunteered?"

He shrugged. "New school. Trying to make friends. Monica wanted me to see her and Amy cheer. Plus . . ." His voice trailed off.

"Plus what?" I asked.

"Wanted to see you in action." He looked away when he said it, almost like he was owning up to something.

"What did you think?"

"Well, I thought that the basket toss Amy and Monica pulled off at halftime was just really top-notch cheer work. Both of them had great extension, and . . ."

Jon saw the look on my face and started giggling like I was a little kid. That's when I realized he was joking and cracked up too. I hadn't been this drunk in a while. "Not *them*, you moron." I punched him lightly in the shoulder. "What did you think of *me*?"

He looked at me like he was sizing me up. "I think I came to the right game."

I tried to hold his gaze, but my face was on fire again, and I looked back up at the house. "So, you and Amy . . . ?" The question hung in the air between us.

He gave a silent laugh—a puff of air somewhere between a chuckle and a sigh. "Your girlfriend seems heavily invested in the idea that Amy and I should go out."

Your girlfriend. Something about those words made me jump to my feet. A knot formed in the pit of my stomach. What was I doing? I am the star of the football team. How long have I been drunk, sitting by a burnt-out bonfire with the new kid? Was Monica looking for me? What would she think if she couldn't find me? Were the guys wondering where I was?

"C'mon. We should go find the girls."

Jon looked up at me sort of startled. "Oh . . . okay. Yeah, sure." He didn't get up. "You okay?" he asked.

"Yeah—I'm fine—just . . . We should get back to the party."

Jon glanced up toward the house, but he didn't move. "You go ahead, man," he said. "I think I'm just gonna sit here for a second. I'm a little dizzy from all that Maker's."

For some reason, it felt very important that Jon come with me. I didn't want to walk away from him, but I couldn't stay down here with him anymore either. I held out my hand. He looked at it, then smiled and grabbed it in an arm-wrestling-style grip. I helped pull him up. He must not have been lying about being sort of dizzy because the momentum of getting to his feet carried him right into me, and I stumbled backward a step as our bodies collided on either side of our clasped hands, our forearms pinned between our chests.

"Whoa!" he said, and grabbed my shoulder with his free hand. I wrapped my arm around him to steady us before we both went tumbling into the hot coals behind us.

We were so close, I could feel the warmth of his breath on my cheek. I could smell his cologne or his deodorant or something—it was sweet and peppery, and his eyes were level with mine. I hadn't realized how tall he was, and his blue eyes had the same effect on me they had that first time I'd seen them in class.

I froze.

We stared at each other for a second.

"You good?" I asked.

The smirk slowly spread across his face. He nodded. "Yeah." He reached down and grabbed the messenger bag that had held the bourbon, tossing the strap nonchalantly over his shoulder and then turning toward the house. "C'mon. Let's go find those cheerleaders."

Later . . .

My hand was about to fall off after writing all that, so I had to take a break. I just read it over, and I'm still not sure how I feel, but maybe it's good to have it down on paper anyway.

Monica called. We're going to grab some food and see a movie tonight. She wanted me to call Jon and see if he wanted to call Amy and invite her, too, and then we could double date. What is it with girls and double dates? I told her I wanted it to be just us tonight. She seemed really pleased to hear that, but I don't think it was because of the same reasons I meant it. There's just something about Jon that makes me feel . . . weird. I get distracted and confused—like I'm not sure what's going on. It's not bad. I had fun last night, but I just . . . I don't know what it is. I guess I feel worried, somehow.

What am I worried about? About being friends with the new kid?

Erin just texted me. Tyler is home from the hospital. I feel like I should call him, but what do I say? That situation makes me feel weird in a whole different way. On top of it all, my stomach still feels queasy from the Maker's last night. I need a couple of cheeseburgers, like, yesterday.

Gonna jump in the shower and go pick up Monica. Have to eat if I'm gonna make it through this movie alive.

Sunday, September 2

Just got home from church. Mom has only two rules about church:

1. I have to go.
2. I have to leave my phone in the truck.

I can drive myself. I can sit wherever I want during the service. I can go out for lunch after with Monica and my friends. Whatever. I just have to go, and I can't surf the Web on my phone. It's boring as hell, but I deal.

Anyway, after the service today, Monica walked me out to my truck, and I turned on my phone while we were hanging out, talking.

There was a text message from a 773 area code that I didn't recognize:

```
Hey man. Jon here. Thanks for hanging
last night. Call me today? Need quote from
you about the game for my blog post.
```

I smiled when I saw it, and Monica asked me who it was from. I told her it was Jon and wondered how he'd gotten my number. She said he'd asked her for it after the game on Friday.

"He's such a great guy," she said. "I'm glad you two hit it off."

She leaned over the console and wrapped a hand around my neck. I felt her dark red nails graze my ear as she pulled me over and kissed me on the lips. She tried to slide her tongue into my mouth, and I pulled back.

"Are you nuts?" I asked.

"What?" she said, all wide-eyed and innocent.

"We're in the church parking lot at high noon."

She rolled her eyes. "Oh, puh-lease. Nobody is looking at us." She turned around and glanced at the front door of the church. Her grandma was walking out with her grandfather. Monica sighed. "Off to Hometown Corral. Home of America's cheapest salad bar." She pecked me on the cheek and jumped out of the truck.

I texted Jon back that I'd call him after lunch.

We just finished eating, and I came up to my room to call him, but I thought I'd write all this down first.

I feel nervous about calling him, but I'm not sure why. Like, I wouldn't feel this way about calling Tyler. Why should I feel this way about calling Jon?

Later . . .

I don't know why I was nervous about calling Jon. That kid had me laughing the second he got me on the phone. He told me

42

that his headline for the blog was going to be "Second-String QB Leaps Tall Buildings in Single Bound," and we ended up talking for, like, forty-five minutes.

He made me promise to send him a country playlist online. Said he needed redneck tunes to inspire his writing about football. I just finished sending him a list on Spotify, mainly classics like George Strait and Garth Brooks—the old stuff.

Jon is hilarious.

Now I've gotta call the Oklahoma scout. Here goes nothing. . . .

Voice mail. She's out of the office until Friday. I left my info.

Monday, September 3
English—First Period

Tyler's back today. I was surprised to see him. For some reason, I thought he'd stay at home or something. Mrs. Harrison got him a chair to prop his foot up on when he came in on his crutches. He's wearing a big white brace that wraps all the way around his left leg with Velcro straps and keeps his knee from bending. I can see it out of the corner of my eye because he sits right behind me. I caught his eye and said, "Hey, man," when he passed my desk. He didn't smile or anything—not that I can blame him. When Tyler gets pissed, you know it.

Tyler. Is. Pissed.

I am really afraid that he's going to be pissed at me

personally. Even though I know it's not my fault. Hell, I even tried to stop him from running that play. It won't matter though. When Tyler gets angry, he doesn't think anything through. He was mad at me one time because I got a better grade on a chemistry test we studied for together last year. He was a total dick to me for a whole week even though he was the one who was texting Erin the whole time I was trying to quiz him about the periodic table. Somehow, when he flunked the test, it was all my fault.

Finally I just told him to screw off. I said, "Dude. It's not my fault you didn't study. It's not my fault you didn't pay attention when I tried to help you. It's not my fault your grade in the class was already in the shitter so flunking one more test got you benched for three games."

And then? Boom. Just like that everything was cool again. He didn't apologize, but when I finally stood up to him, he backed off.

I hate feeling like that's going to happen again.

Of course, Monica would say that it *isn't* happening again. Not yet anyway. She's always going on about how people worry all the time about what's going to happen in the future so it ruins what is happening right this second. She's always writing LITN in big letters on stuff—her notebooks, sticky notes in her locker, under her name when she signs somebody's yearbook; online it's her hash tag for almost everything: #LITN. *Live in the now.*

I guess I'm not so good with that. I like to be prepared for what's coming next. It's why I work so hard in practice and even write plays out sometimes. Nothing is worse than a moment on the field where you get taken by surprise—where you don't see it coming. It's called getting blindsided for a reason.

Crap . . .

Joy Lucht just came in late and was walking to her seat behind Tyler's desk. She accidentally bumped the chair his foot is propped up on with her purse, and Tyler shrieked and cussed a blue streak. Dropped an f-bomb in the middle of class. Everybody froze.

Joy was tripping over herself to apologize, and Mrs. Harrison calmly walked down the row and told her to sit, that it would be okay. Tyler was red in the face. He threw his notebook on the ground and yelled that it would *not* be "f-ing" okay, only he said it. He actually *said it again*. In class. To a teacher.

The only person I would rather not piss off in the entire universe besides Tyler is Mrs. Harrison. She stood very still right next to Tyler's desk, just behind my left shoulder, for what seemed like a very long time. She was giving him the kind of look that turned animals to stone in Narnia. "Have you lost your mind?"

Tyler crossed his arms and looked in the other direction.

"Excuse me. I am speaking to you." Mrs. Harrison has this way of saying things when she demands to be heard that is . . .

well, terrifying. She very rarely speaks in this manner, so when she does, it is generally very impressive. It's not loud, exactly. In fact, it's less a matter of volume and more a matter of tone.

Even Tyler was no match for it. He turned and looked at her.

"I asked you a question, sir. Have you lost your mind?"

"No." Tyler's voice was tight like a spring being stretched.

"No . . . what?" Mrs. Harrison was not backing down.

"No, ma'am."

"I am happy to hear that, Tyler, because I need you to muster the strength of every spare neuron you have to rub together and make sure that this next thing I'm going to tell you registers very deeply in your central nervous system. I want to make sure that this next statement I make is something you understand at a cellular level. So, are you listening? Do I have your attention?"

"Yes, ma'am."

"Good. Now hear this: One more outburst or use of language like that in my classroom and the world of pain I will rain down on you will be the stuff of legend. I am very sorry that you were hurt on Friday night, and I know it is very upsetting to face the prospect of losing your senior season of football to an injury. I understand that Joy here bumped your leg, and I know that must have hurt very badly. But understand that if you disrespect my classroom, or your fellow classmates, with the use of profanity in that manner ever again, I will call your mother and the principal so quickly that the pain you're in now will feel like a day at Disneyland."

She turned around and spread her arms out, indicating all of us.

"How many of you were at the ball game on Friday night?" she asked. Almost everyone in the room raised a hand. Mrs. Harrison nodded. "Good, good," she said. "And how many of you would be willing to help Tyler get around?" Every hand in the class was raised.

"Tyler, this will not be easy, but at any moment, at any time, there is an entire room full of very able people—several of whom I know for a fact care for you quite deeply—who are at the ready to help. The decision to ask for that help, and to allow yourself to be loved through a difficult time, is yours, but from this moment on, you must understand that to do things the hard way is something you have volunteered for—not something that is necessary. Do you understand me?"

I heard Tyler let out a long, slow sigh behind me. "I don't need help getting around. I need help keeping my scholarship offer."

Mrs. Harrison nodded. "I understand your concern, Tyler. I have no answer for you there. I do not know what your prognosis will be, and only time will tell if you'll keep that scholarship or not. You don't have a single iota of control over that. However, there is something that you *do* have control over, and that is whether you conduct yourself through a difficult and trying time with the dignity and grace of a young man of character, or whether you will wallow in the misery of being a victim." She picked up Tyler's notebook and pen and placed them back on his desk. "It is my sincere hope that you will choose the former, and not the latter."

Mrs. Harrison walked past me back to the front of the room and glanced at the clock, then told us to write in our journals for another five minutes. Jon glanced over at me and raised his eyebrows like, *Holy. Crap.*

Mrs. Harrison is incredible.

(So are Jon's eyes. I know I keep saying that. I just keep . . . noticing.)

Study Hall—Fifth Period

I am so pissed off right now, I can barely hold this pen. For some reason, I thought that speech Mrs. Harrison gave Tyler this morning would mellow him the hell out, but I should've known better.

Getting Tyler down the hall to the cafeteria for lunch took some time, so I helped him get situated at our usual table. Brandon Sears, Corey Tracker, and Mike Watters were all there, and Erin went through the cafeteria line and got him some food. She came back with Tyler's tray right as Monica and Amy walked up with Jon.

Sears immediately grinned and gave Jon a high five. "There's the Music Man with the Maker's. Dang, boy. That party was off the hook."

Tracker moved his backpack so Jon could sit, and I smiled and held out my fist for a bump across the table. Jon sort of glanced down at my hand and then grinned as he bumped back.

"Music Man?" As we all sat down, Tyler was squinting at Jon like he was trying to make out the shape of an alien life-form. Immediately I was wary.

"Yep," Monica chirped. "Jon and I met at the auditions for the fall musical on Friday. Cast list goes up tomorrow. He's got an amazing voice."

Tyler groaned. "Jesus. Leave you alone for a weekend and you start hanging out with the fags."

My stomach dropped when he said this, and everybody at the table froze. The word "fags" landed like a bomb in the middle of the table, and I felt my face go beet red and my mind go blank. I'd heard guys on the team call each other that all the time. I've said it a bunch—mainly so that nobody would suspect anything about me. But something about hearing Tyler say it about Jon—my heart is racing again right now just writing it down. And was he just saying it about Jon?

Or was he talking about me?

There was this glint in Tyler's eyes that seemed to dare me to say something. Both of my fists clenched, and I had this flash where I envisioned flipping his tray full of food into his face, then bashing him across the head with it. Before I could move, Monica was on her feet, yelling.

I was so angry, I couldn't really hear what she was saying. I caught certain phrases: *Asshole . . . How would you know . . . Such a dick . . . Shut the hell up . . .* I could hear the blood pounding in my ears, and it was like everything was in slow motion. I looked at Jon, and he was staring down at his food. Then his eyes floated up to meet mine. I held his gaze for what felt like a long time, until I heard Monica say:

"Besides. He's going out with Amy."

Her words were like a foghorn through the blur, and Jon frowned as he glanced over at Monica, then down at the table, but not back at me. I don't know why, but I hated Monica so much in that moment, the way she's always got everything figured out and everyone labeled and paired off and arranged so neatly into our places in her universe, where we constantly orbit her star.

Watters whistled low under his breath when Monica's tirade finally screeched to a halt. Tracker looked like he was about to start laughing his ass off, and Sears just shook his head and said, "Well. I guess she told *you*, big man." There was a moment of silence, and then Tracker finally burst out laughing. The tension dissipated as everybody around the table joined in.

Except for me.

And Tyler.

And Jon.

Tyler glared at Monica. Then his eyes narrowed in Jon's direction. He opened his mouth to say something, but I jumped in before he could.

"Jon, this is Tyler. Tyler, this is Jon. He sits across the aisle from us in Harrison's class."

Jon held out a hand to shake Tyler's. Tyler stared at it for a second, then reached over, and they shook. "I've seen him," Tyler said slowly. "I just didn't know he'd infiltrated our lunch table."

"What, do you work for the CIA now?" Watters asked.

Sears shook his head. "Ease up on the white boy, tiger. If it hadn't been for him, I'd have been stuck drinking that bong water beer at the party on Friday."

Jon gave Tyler a tentative smile. "Good game Friday. Sorry about your knee."

Tyler snorted. "What were *you* doing at the football game?" He wasn't giving an inch.

"Jesus, Ty. It's a free country. He can go to a football game

51

at his own high school." Erin rolled her eyes and smiled at Jon. "Sorry. He's not usually like this."

"Yes, he is." Monica muttered this as she pulled open her yogurt. She was having none of it. "Jon was covering the season opener for *The Battalion*."

"The *what*?" Tyler asked.

"The school newspaper." Amy had been silent, sitting next to Jon, but she jumped in with a smile. She kept stealing glances at Jon, who was keeping his eyes on his lunch for the most part. I could feel the weight of the tension in the air between Jon and Tyler. Jon had been doing that thing where you don't look a snarling dog in the eye, but he put down his sandwich and turned to face Tyler head-on.

"It's mainly a blog now," Jon explained to Tyler. "They only print three issues each year. Paper, labor, and shipping cost a lot more than posting it on the Web. Besides, who reads newspapers anymore?"

"So did you write up the big game?" Tyler sneered this, and I felt the muscles between my shoulder blades tighten. God, he is such a dick sometimes. For some reason, because his surliness was not directed at me, but instead at somebody new, I felt it more acutely. I stared laser beams through him across the table, but his sights were set on Jon. Was he always this big a douche bag, but I just never noticed? What is it about Jon that makes me so pissed off when Tyler talks to him this way?

Jon ignored the tone of Tyler's voice and answered the question as if Tyler had asked sincerely. "Sure did. Great game. You two really nailed that handoff play."

"Yeah, it wasn't so great from the emergency room."

Jon pursed his lips, then took a deep breath and tried again. "Yeah, that part sucked. Again, really sorry about that, dude."

"You and me both." Tyler cracked open the can of Coke that Erin had brought him and took a swallow, then belched loudly.

"Wow, Tyler. Classy." Monica sighed, and Erin glanced around, embarrassed.

Tyler ignored them both. "And what qualifies you to write about football . . . *dude?*"

My stomach was in knots. I wanted to brain Tyler, but I felt paralyzed. I couldn't even speak. I felt like an SUV was parked on my chest. I could barely get a breath. It was like I was watching a car wreck in slow motion.

Jon shrugged. "Just like football, I guess. My older brother played in high school. Went to all his games."

"And where was that?"

"Chicago." It came out sounding all choked and mangled, but at least I was finally able to say something.

Tyler turned and looked at me like he'd forgotten I was there. He raised his eyebrows. "Got a Yankee in our midst," he crowed, then turned back to Jon. "You ever *play* football?"

Jon shook his head as he swallowed the last bite of his sandwich. "Nah—not much for team sports."

"Just like to *watch*, huh?"

"He's on the swim team," I offered. It seemed very important to me to make Tyler aware that Jon was an athlete. Why do I feel like I have to defend Jon to Tyler? Why is it so important to me that Tyler like him?

The minute I said it, I knew it was a mistake. Tyler's eyes narrowed again, and he snorted. "The *swim team*? Oh, great." He was about to say more, but mercifully Tracker broke in.

"Oh yeah—I meant to tell you, my sister's on the girls swim team." He smiled at Jon around a mouthful of mystery meat. I hadn't touched mine yet. "I forgot to tell you at the bonfire on Friday."

Sears laughed. "Yeah, 'cause your skinny ass was drunk off two tugs on that bottle of bourbon."

Jon saw his escape and took it. He wadded up his brown paper lunch sack and slipped the strap of his messenger bag over his head so it crossed his chest.

"Where are you going?" Monica asked.

"Gotta post the story about the game after school. Need to get it approved by Miss Howerton next period and gotta make a few edits. Catch you guys later."

I tried to catch his eye as he turned and walked out of the cafeteria, but he didn't look at me.

That's the worst part of this whole fiasco. I bet Jon's mad at me for not standing up to Tyler. I'll bet he thinks I'm a total tool now. Some dumb jock who runs around the locker room snapping towels and calling people "fag."

Why do I care? Why do I feel so worked up about this? Am I mad at Tyler, or am I pissed off at myself? What do I have to be angry about? Maybe I'm not angry at all. Maybe I've just gotten a glimpse of what Tyler is really like from somebody else's point of view.

Maybe I'm just scared. Scared that my best friend is an idiot. Scared that he knows about me. Scared that everything I've worked so hard to build for myself is about to come spilling out—over what? This freaking new kid?

I can't let that happen.

Tuesday, September 4
6:30 a.m.

Woke up an hour ago and couldn't get back to sleep. I was dreaming about Jon running down a football field that never seemed to end. He was being chased by Tyler, and I was watching from the stands. In the dream, I knew that if Tyler tackled Jon, something terrible would happen. I was trying to get down onto the field to run in between them, to tackle Tyler before he got to Jon, but there was a huge chain-link fence all the way around the field with razor wire at the top, and each time I tried to climb it, I cut myself.

I woke up sweating, with my heart racing.

Turns out Jon needs zero help from me defending himself. He posted his blog about our first football game right after school yesterday. I don't remember ever hearing anybody talk about going online to read *The Battalion* before, but by the time I was walking out of practice yesterday, like, fifteen people had texted me about it.

In the write-up, Jon called what was happening on the field Friday before Tyler got sacked "a slaughter." He wrote that the only decent play Tyler pulled off was the fake out to me, and even that he managed to do only once before getting permanently sidelined. He wrote that everybody in the stands breathed a sigh of relief when I took the field and started nailing pass after pass. He ended with a comment about "the injured QB cussing a blue streak this morning in English class."

I decided to try to head this one off at the pass. I had a hunch Tyler hadn't read it yet, and after practice, I drove straight to his house. His mom opened the door and gave me a hug. Downstairs in his room, I waited while Tyler read the article. Then he turned to me and said, "Dude. Why did you tell me to read that?"

I told him because I wanted him to hear about it from me.

He just shrugged. "Whatever, man."

"What do you mean, 'Whatever'?" I asked him.

He stared at the screen of his laptop for a long time and then flipped it closed. "It's all true."

"So . . ."

"So what?" he said.

"So you're not mad?"

He shook his head once and snorted. Then he picked up one of his crutches and yelled louder than I have ever heard him yell as he threw it against the door of his bedroom. The foam part of the crutch that goes under your arm splintered a hole in the cheap paneled door and stuck there.

I had never seen Tyler cry before last night. He didn't even try to hide it; he just sat there and sobbed like people do on TV when somebody's mom dies or something. Tyler's mom was very certainly not dead, and she came running down the stairs, calling his name. When she burst through the door, the crutch fell out of the hole it had made and wedged itself down behind the door, effectively keeping her out. I finally wrangled the door open, and she just stood there, staring. She walked toward Tyler and tried to touch his face and his shoulder, and he just shrugged her off, then grabbed a pillow and yelled into it.

His mom smoothed his bangs out of his face and said, "I'm

so sorry, son." He pulled away from her again, and she turned and smiled sadly at me as she slowly walked toward the door. "You're a good friend to come over and check on him."

The truth is, I feel like the worst friend of all. I'm the one who benefits from Tyler's injury. I'm the one who is all worried about what the kid who wrote this blog post thinks of me. What would Tyler do if he knew that every time I close my eyes I see the hem of Jon's T-shirt riding up his stomach? What would his mom say?

She wouldn't think I was such a great friend then, would she? Maybe I'm not.

After she left the room, I sat down on the bed next to Tyler. I reached over and gave his shoulder a squeeze. He shrugged my hand away.

"Dude. Get off me. Just get outta here."

"What?" I asked. "So you're just gonna push away everybody who tries to help you?"

"What the hell can you do to help me, man? What can my *mom* do? Jack shit. That's what everybody can do."

I sat there, feeling helpless. I wanted to run and get as far away from Tyler as I could. He felt lethal at that moment—like he might explode and take me with him.

"I can just . . . be here." I said it so quietly, I wasn't sure he heard me.

He did.

"Wouldn't you rather be off somewhere with New Jon?" he scoffed.

"What?"

"You heard me," he snarled.

"Tyler, you've been my best friend since seventh grade. Jesus."

He wiped the back of his hand under his nose, and his cheek across the shoulder of his shirt. Then he looked right at me. His eyes were rimmed with red and puffy from crying.

"Really? Have I been?" he asked.

I frowned. "What the hell are you talking about, dude? Of course."

He narrowed his eyes at me. "I'm not sure I even know who you are."

My heart started racing. The beat was thumping out *He knows He knows He knows* against my rib cage. He was saying it without saying it.

I tried to laugh it off—like every other time Tyler was ever a hothead, like every other time he'd lost his temper and thrown his fist against a locker or a putter against the mini golf green.

"Christ." I rolled my eyes. "Nice drama, dude. They should cast you in that damn musical."

Tyler stayed quiet, so I reached over and grabbed the crutch he'd thrown and leaned it up against the wall beside his bed. "Dad got me a new rifle for my birthday. Come over on Saturday. Let's try it out and hang."

I don't really care that much about hunting, but Dad's a big deer hunter, and it's something we've always done together. Usually Dad shuts down his construction business for the first week of the season in November and takes Tyler and me out for a few nights. We sleep in a tent, and he lets us have a couple of beers when we're sitting around the campfire.

"I can't even drive," Tyler said. "I have to have surgery the end of this month anyway. No way I can go hunting with you guys."

"Have Erin drive you over," I said. "Monica's stopping by after rehearsal. We'll chill. It'll be normal—like it was before all . . . this."

I was headed for the door when his voice stopped me: "Don't you get it?" Something about his tone stopped me midstride. I turned around and saw his eyes on fire. A chill ran down my spine. "It'll never be like it was," he said quietly. "This changes everything."

I don't remember driving home, or dinner, really. I stayed awake last night for a long time thinking about what Tyler meant by that remark.

I'm certain he wasn't talking about football.

He was talking about us.

Wednesday, September 5
English—First Period

Mr. London, the drama teacher and choir director, posted the cast list for *The Music Man* yesterday right before lunch. The minute the bell rang in chemistry, Monica dragged me down the hall, practically running. The list was hanging on the bulletin boards outside of the choir room. We were the first ones there, and Monica started shrieking like a banshee. As she jumped up and down and was swarmed by half the cheerleading squad, I leaned in to read the list:

Hillside High Fall Musical Cast List—*The Music Man*

Harold Hill—Jon Statley

Marian Paroo—Monica Weaver

The whole cast was listed below that, but as I was reading, I felt somebody leaning over my shoulder to see the names. It had gotten crowded fast once the bell rang. People were jostling, and Monica was still jumping up and down, shrieking, but for some reason, I knew who it was.

I just ... *knew*. It was so weird. That's never happened to me before.

I turned my head slightly to the right for a glance, and Jon's face was right there, his chin hovering over my shoulder. I hadn't ever realized that he's maybe an inch or so taller than I am. His face was really close to mine, and it sort of scared me. I turned my head to face the list again so my lips weren't, like, an inch from his cheek, but I couldn't really go anywhere because people were crowding around and knocking into us in their excitement. Somebody elbowed us, and I felt Jon put his hand on my back so he could catch his balance—but then he just kept it there.

I don't even know why I'm writing this down. Mrs. Harrison put on the board today that the topic was SOMETHING MEMORABLE, and I thought I'd write about Monica seeing her name on the cast list. I guess if I'm completely honest, her reaction wasn't the most memorable part of that moment. How is Jon touching me the thing I remember the most in the last forty-eight hours?

I can feel it all again—like it's happening right this second. We are just standing there in a river of people, pinned in by all these bodies, eyes locked on that damn board. In the middle of the ruckus, the two of us just stood there, still—motionless— like boulders in rapids, people bouncing off of us, left and right. I stared straight ahead at the list, not really reading the words, his hand on my back. We stayed that way for what? Two, three seconds tops. It seemed like so much longer.

I can still feel the heat of his palm where his fingers rested—just beneath my right shoulder blade.

Finally I turned my head again and said, "You did it."

He glanced at me with a big smile, and I knew it was going to be okay between us. We hadn't really talked this week—since that whole thing with Tyler at lunch on Monday and the post about the game. I saw him every morning in English, but he didn't hang around to talk. He'd always jet out while I was helping Tyler juggle books and crutches.

Tyler's been sort of quiet since we talked at his place after Jon's post went up, and I feel like I need to patch things up with him somehow. I've been helping him get from class to class a lot—making sure he's got his books and crap. I just don't want him to think . . .

Shit.

I mean . . . what? What don't I want him to think?

That I'm a fag?

That I'm into Jon?

What if both of those things are true? I don't want my best friend to know the truth about me? I hate this limbo. After what Tyler said to me on Monday about things never being the same again, I'm pretty sure he knows. Or suspects.

What would it be like if Tyler knew who I *really* was? What if he knew that yesterday when I stood in front of the cast list at the water fountain and Jon put his hand on my back, my knees went weak like I'd been running line drills across the football field for a month?

It was like no sensation I'd ever had before; it was what I know Tyler talks about when he tells me stories about hooking up with Erin. Even the first time Monica and I got naked together, I didn't feel a jolt course through me like I did from just the touch of Jon's hand on my back in the hallway. Standing there yesterday, I felt like my legs might buckle underneath me at any moment, and somehow at the same time I knew that as long as Jon was there, no one could ever knock me down.

Later . . .

Big write-up in the *Democrat-Gazette* yesterday about the game last week—picture of me and everything. The reporter mentioned the scouts who were there to recruit Tyler, who was "felled early on by an injury," and how they were "pleasantly surprised" by my "seasoned passing game."

Mom had gone to buy five extra copies of the paper and had one spread out on the table while she put one into a scrapbook and stuffed envelopes with the other clippings for Grandma and Grandpa in Dallas. Dad whooped and squeezed me into a big bear hug when I walked through the door.

"You're gonna get that full ride to Oklahoma! You're the

man!" He was red-faced and had the skunky smell of a man who was three beers into a celebration already, but it was fun to see him excited.

"There's a YouTube video of that big pass you made, and it already has more than seven thousand views." Little sisters are notoriously hard to impress—especially when they're in eighth grade—but YouTube hits are apparently the ticket.

"Have you heard from that woman who was at the game on Friday yet, sweetheart?" Mom handed me a warm plate of meat loaf and potatoes au gratin—my favorite kind out of the box. She made them special for me.

I smiled. "This looks great. And no, not yet. I left her a voice mail on Sunday, but her message said she'd be away until Friday."

"You'll hear from her now," Dad said, a little too loudly. Sometimes when he gets buzzed, it's like the volume gets turned up too loud, and it drives me a little nuts. But not tonight. He beamed at me from the end of the table. "You're golden."

Thursday, September 6

It's actually after midnight on Thursday night. I guess it's technically Friday morning. I have been lying in bed for, like, two hours and can't sleep.

Monica and Jon were waiting for me at my truck this

afternoon when I was done with practice. Monica was talking one hundred miles per hour to Jon. She had her arm laced through his and was sort of hanging on him and laughing. It was weird because if it were anybody else, I might have felt jealous. Or at least had the idea that I should feel jealous. But not Jon. He was just leaning against the side of the truck, listening to Monica, but staring over her head right at me.

Sometimes there are these moments when I feel like I'm living a movie version of my own life. The sun was setting, and a breeze carried the smell of cut grass off the field. Something about all that and Jon's gaze—as still and calm as Monica was animated and boisterous—made me feel this weird sense of excitement and relief all at once. Something about the way he looks at me makes me feel like I'm invincible.

Monica turned and saw me and came running up. She threw her arms around my neck and never stopped talking about their first rehearsal and how great Jon was and how much fun this is going to be, and on and on and on. . . .

And the whole time she talked, I just smiled and held Jon's gaze.

Monica's great—don't get me wrong. I just . . . I don't even know how to write it down. . . .

I just feel this thing when Jon is looking at me with those eyes. It's like he sucks me into a freaking mind meld. I couldn't even hear anything Monica was saying—something about . . . I don't even remember. I forgot all about being worried about the quiz and tonight's game and whether Tyler can tell I'm into Jon or not. As I stood there at the truck with the clouds turning neon orange, I just knew that everything was going to work out, that as long as Jon was looking at me, everything was going to be okay.

Monica finally stopped and realized neither one of us was listening to her.

"What?"

I glanced down at her. "Huh?"

"Do I have something in my teeth?" she asked, suddenly panicked. She whirled and playfully smacked Jon on the shoulder. "Um. You're supposed to *tell* me. . . ." She ducked around me and peered into the side mirror on the cab.

Jon shook his head, laughing. "You're beautiful, crazy." Then he winked at me. "How was football practice?"

"Brutal. How was play practice?"

He arched an eyebrow. "It's *rehearsal*. Only Philistines call it 'play practice.'"

"I *am* the quarterback of the football team."

"Philistine." He sighed. "We're gonna have to get you some culture." His look of pity dissolved into a smirk that made me feel like I'd just popped over the top of a steep hill driving a little too fast.

"Fine, but first I need some food. And what the hell with this chemistry quiz?"

We wound up studying for the quiz together. I texted my mom and let her know I was having dinner with Monica and Jon so we could study. We went to IHOP and got a booth in the back. I ordered a burger and a stack of pancakes with strawberries and whipped cream. Somehow, between the two of them, they drilled the noble gasses and halogens from the periodic table into my head.

Afterward there was this weird moment when we headed into the parking lot. Monica gave Jon a big hug and said, "See you tomorrow," then grabbed my hand and kind of waited. I saw this look pass over Jon's face, and he nodded—sort of like he knew this was where he should say good night, but he didn't want to leave.

Something flipped in my stomach right then—this weird knot of . . . what? Stress? Panic? I couldn't tell what was happening. I just got . . . annoyed. With Monica. Of all things. Suddenly I felt miffed that I had to walk her to her car instead of walking Jon down to his. I even started to take a step toward him, but then I caught myself:

What the hell are you doing, dude? Monica is your girlfriend.

It was Tyler's voice in my brain. Calling me out.

I turned bright red. I could feel it happening. I was trying to cover, but I could tell Jon had caught this weird start-stop moment, and I didn't know what to do. I put out an arm, sorta like I was going to hug him, but then stopped myself halfway through the motion, which was like this weird fumble. He sort of leaned in when he saw me raise my arm, and then stopped when I did, and finally he held out his hand, and we freaking shook hands. Which . . . I mean . . . Nothing could have been more awkward than that.

I kicked myself all the way back to the car, Monica talking ninety-to-nothing about . . . what? I don't even know. All I could see was the smirk on Jon's face as I turned away to walk Monica through the parking lot. I finally got her to her car, and she wanted to make out, but I told her I had to get home. We kissed a couple times, but I couldn't stop thinking that Jon was gonna see us, and . . .

And what? Why did I give a shit if Jon saw us? I leaned in to Monica, pressing her up against the side of the car, and kissed her nice and hard. I could taste the watermelon lip gloss she'd just reapplied, and her mouth was fruity and soft and wet and warm, and for some reason, I just thought, *This is like kissing Jell-O.*

That made me laugh, and she pulled away and started laughing too. "What?" she asked.

"Nothing." I shook my head. "Sorry. That lip gloss tastes like Jolly Ranchers."

She giggled and flipped her hair over her shoulder. "I have delicious lips."

I watched her drive away and felt my phone buzz in my hip pocket. I pulled it out and there was a text from Jon:

```
Nice lip-lock. ;)
```

My heart sped up when I read it. I tapped out a single-word reply on the screen; then my thumbs froze for a second over Send. Finally I hit it. The word popped up in a little green bubble on the screen:

```
Jealous?
```

I almost couldn't breathe while I waited for his response. I could see that he was texting something back, and my hands got so sweaty, I almost dropped my phone. Two seconds later, his response came through:

```
Maybe a little. ;)
```

I laughed out loud in my truck, and I couldn't stop smiling all the way home. I don't even know how to explain how weird it felt—how happy I was.

And how scared that makes me.

I mean, if Tyler or my dad or my mom, or . . . well . . . anybody, really . . . saw my phone and read those texts, they'd know that I was flirting. With a guy. Was he serious?

Am I?

I haven't responded again to Jon's text, but I want to. I want to feel the rush of waiting for his reply. It feels dangerous—like I'm a little out of control.

Okay, here it is: the truth . . . Shit. I can't believe I'm gonna write this down.

The truth is, I've been lying here awake 'cause I can't stop thinking about pushing Jon up against my truck and kissing him instead of Monica. What would that feel like? What would it be like to kiss a dude? It wouldn't taste like watermelon—that much I know for sure. I even went online and searched "boys kissing." Some of the videos that popped up were just guys horsing around being stupid, and some of them were kind of gross, but there was one of these two guys on a beach. They looked like they were about my age, and they were just sitting in this big tidal pool making out as the waves rolled in behind them. It made my heart speed up the way that getting Jon's text tonight did. These dudes didn't seem like they were afraid of getting caught, or of anybody seeing them. They were just kissing each other like it was the most normal thing in the world.

I can't stop thinking about what it would be like to feel Jon's lips on mine now. And it's, like, one a.m. and I really need to get to sleep, or I'm so screwed for the game tomorrow.

Friday, September 7
English—First Period

Holy crap. I was up way too late last night.

When I finally drifted off to sleep, I had another dream. Only this time, instead of Tyler chasing Jon, he was chasing me down the football field. I was running as fast as I could, but the end zone kept getting farther and farther away. I looked back, and Tyler was chasing me with a crutch that he held up like a rifle and started shooting at me.

I'm so tired today, I'm not sure how I'm going to make it to the game tonight. When I saw Jon this morning, he just grinned and tossed his chin at me, like *What's up?* He didn't say anything about our texts. Maybe he was just joking around. Maybe I was too. Then why am I having these whacked-out dreams about Tyler? And why can't I stop thinking about Jon? And what if I walk out on the field and choke? What if last Friday was a fluke?

I can't afford to be this tired. Coach is always after us: "Keep your head in the game." My head is everywhere *but* the game right now.

What the hell am I doing?

Saturday, September 8

I am writing this from hell.

Actually, it's my bedroom, but Tracy just downloaded the new Boison album. Get it? Like "Poison" only they're "Deadly to Boys," as the title track has reminded me for the past thirty-two minutes. They're this sixteen-year-old girl group that came from some TV show for kids, and they sing the worst pop singles of all time. They're fast and stupid, and have terrible lyrics. They sound just like the color hot pink. You can totally picture eighth-grade girls jumping up and down and screaming along. The track Tracy is singing to right now has this awful chorus about how some dude is "the one I've always wanted," and they say that like five hundred times in a row. She's had this album on repeat for two days now. I'm about to lose my shit.

Anyway, in better news, we beat Central High last night. Didn't choke. We were up by three at the half, but it could've gone either way. I got sacked twice really hard the first two plays of the second half, and on the second one, the ball got away from me. Somehow the defensive lineman from the other team who was closest to the ball kicked it as he scrambled for it, and I grabbed it—but I got piled on pretty hard.

That put us at third and fourteen on our own forty-yard line. I was not feeling good about it. If we had to punt, I knew

Central would score, and I knew we'd give up the momentum. The hardest thing in football isn't scoring. It's keeping the momentum. Getting the ball down the field when you're behind because you had to punt is somehow twice as hard. The number of yards to the end zone is the exact same as if you're ahead, but the challenge is all between your ears, as Coach likes to say, and it feels like trying to run through knee-deep mud.

I knew we had to make the first down or we'd be in serious shit.

Walker, our center, smacked my helmet when we came out of the huddle and just said, "You got this."

And I realized he was right. I could do this.

He snapped me the ball, and I dropped back. For some reason, our line was screwed, and none of my guys were where I needed them to be. I saw the same dude who had kicked the ball on the last play break free and barrel toward me. I took a couple steps to my right, ready to run for it, but just those two steps to the right gave me a whole new view of the field, and I saw Mike Watters wide open way down on their ten.

It's a weird thing to just be in the moment and act on instinct. I'd never completed a pass quite that long before. If I'd had the time to consider that, I'd have psyched myself out. I didn't have time to think about it—I just knew it was right. So I cocked my arm and let it rip.

I watched the ball arc down the field in a perfect spiral. I don't know if the crowd actually went silent, or if I just couldn't hear them, but when Mike Watters reached out and got his hands on that pass, the whole stadium exploded, and I wound up on the bottom of a pile again. This time it was my own guys, roaring louder than the crowd. We scored one more touchdown after that, and then I got Casey, our kicker, in field-goal range with a minute left and he kicked a thirty-yard field goal as the clock ran out. That's what I mean about momentum. That pass sealed the deal for us. It wasn't even the points. It was the power of knowing that we were in charge.

After the game, Jon was waiting with Monica and Amy. Monica ran up and hugged me. She and Amy were hoarse from cheering. I saw Erin and Tyler were a little bit behind them. It was slow going with Tyler on his crutches, his leg wrapped in a big white Velcro sheath to keep his knee from bending.

Jon held up a hand for a high five. I smiled and smacked it. "Hey, man."

"What's up, ace?" he said. "Nice pass." Something about the way he was smiling let me know he'd seen that moment with the pass—that split second before I saw Watters down the field and the split second after.

"Thanks." I smiled back at him.

"You know how to give a guy something to write about," he said. "This game is another great story for the paper."

Tyler and Erin had made it over by that point, and Tyler snorted. "It's so freaking gay to come to a football game to write about it for the school paper."

When Tyler said "gay" like that, it was like somebody had knocked the wind out of me. I opened my mouth to say something, but nothing came out.

Monica, of course, is never at a loss for words. She turned to Tyler with her patented withering look and said, "Hey, douche bag. He wasn't just here for the paper. In fact, I'm not sure how he's going to write that article. Most of the time he was watching Amy cheer."

Erin and Amy giggled like, well, schoolgirls. As they did, Jon flinched. Nobody else would have noticed it.

But I did.

I'm not sure about much of anything these days, but I'm sure that Jon wasn't watching Amy cheer.

At that moment, this guy came up and tapped me on the shoulder, and I recognized Roger Jackson from his column in the sports section of the paper.

"Great game." He smiled. "Can I get a couple comments from you?"

I knew Monica wanted us all to go out, but when Roger showed up, Jon said he had to go.

"Yeah, I gotta get Erin home." Tyler had this look on his face when he said it and was staring at Roger. It was so weird, like we all had this awkward thought at the exact same moment: *This should be Tyler's interview. If he hadn't gotten hurt, he'd be the one talking to reporters.*

He left to "get Erin home," which I didn't realize until right now is sad and funny at the same time because she has to drive them everywhere now—but he said his knee was hurting anyway.

I watched Jon head across the parking lot as Roger asked me how it felt to complete that pass.

"How did it feel?" I blinked at him. "Is that a trick question?"

He laughed. "You're right. I assume it felt great."

"Hell yeah," I said.

"Was it luck?"

I shrugged. "I guess we'll find out next week."

Again, Roger smiled as he scribbled a couple notes down, then held out his hand. "Thanks for talking with me. See you next Friday."

I shook his hand, and as he turned to leave, he glanced over his shoulder. "Nice work out there. You really see the field."

When he was gone, that left me, Monica, and Amy. Amy said she didn't want to feel like a third wheel, so we all walked to the parking lot, and Amy took off.

At that point, Monica was all smiles. "Looks like I get you all to myself tonight. Finally!"

I smiled and tried to get excited about that idea, but my heart wasn't in it, and she could tell.

"You okay?" she asked.

"Just tired."

"You need me to kiss it and make it better?" she said, wrapping her arms around my neck and pressing her whole body up against mine.

"I think I need to get home," I said.

She pouted and sighed. "Jeez. So much for a wild Friday night your senior year."

"I'm sorry, babe. I'm just beat."

She raised her eyebrow and smirked. "It's okay," she said. "I'm coming over tomorrow to watch you play with your gun."

I'd forgotten until right then about the whole plan for today. She should be here any minute.

Later . . .

Sometimes I start to write in this journal and I'm sure that I'm losing my freaking mind. If you'd told me two weeks ago that Tyler wouldn't want to stay for dinner when my mom offered, I'd have assumed you were smoking crack. But that's exactly what happened tonight. Tyler is crazy about my mom's cooking. His dad remarried after his mom left when he was a kid, and his stepmom is what I like to call "kitchen-challenged." So, usually, anytime he comes over, I suspect he's sort of coming to hang out with me but mainly coming for my mom's cooking.

He and Erin showed up a few minutes before Monica. Tyler talked with my dad, looking at my new rifle while Erin and I walked the fence row behind our place, setting up some old coffee cans we use for target practice. There's a big meadow that a developer owns but never developed behind our house and then a line of trees along the steep drop that leads down to the river. We can shoot these cans without worrying about hitting anybody by mistake because you can see anybody coming from our backyard for about a quarter mile before the trees start at the river.

Erin and I were talking about Tyler and when his surgery was set to be scheduled. She looked up toward the house and said, "Monica's here." I turned around and saw Monica. Then my heart crashed into my toes when I saw Jon step out of the back door onto our deck, nodding and talking with my mom.

What is he doing here?

At that moment Erin started up toward the house and then looked at me and said, "What?"

I said, "What?" back.

She laughed. "You have this big grin on your face. The one you get before you crack a joke."

I just shrugged, but I realized she was right, and that made me even more nervous and giddy at the same time. I remembered our flirty texts, and I was so happy that Jon was here, but I was nervous about what Tyler would say. And what about my dad? This had the potential to be a total shit show.

And I was grinning like an idiot. And I couldn't stop.

I marched up toward the house with Erin. Monica skipped over from where she was talking with my dad and Tyler and hugged me. She pecked me on the lips and squeaked, "Surprise!"

I looked up at Jon, who was smiling at something my mom said. Mom turned to me and said, "Sweetheart! You didn't tell me about your new friend."

I nodded. "Sorry. Slipped my mind." I smiled at Jon. "Welcome to our humble abode."

This made his lips purse and twist into that smirk he has that makes me weak in the knees. Why do I feel like such a rock star when I make that smirk happen?

"Sorry to show up unannounced," he said.

I shrugged. "The more the merrier."

Mom had disappeared inside and returned with Cokes, a big plate of cheese and crackers, and a platter of cookies. She tapped the screen of her iPhone, and the wireless speakers Dad had rigged up outside sprang to life with the satellite station of old-school country classics that was Dad's favorite. Mom is like the most practical version of Martha Stewart ever. On speed.

Tyler took the first turn with the new rifle. He was off balance because of the crutches and kept hitting the fence post just below the cans. I could see him getting red in the face, and my dad was not helping matters by teasing him.

"C'mon, Ty. Just 'cause you banged up your knee doesn't mean you can shoot like a chick."

Monica marched up at that point and eased the rifle away from Tyler. "Excuse me, Tyler. Mr. Morris, you might want to see how a 'chick' does it. Take notes."

She turned around and promptly blew a coffee can to smithereens. My mom whistled and cheered.

"Attagirl, Monica. Don't you let him tell you what you can't do."

Dad turned to Jon. "So, you new around here?"

Jon nodded. "Yep."

"How'd you meet this motley crew?"

The very thought that my dad was having a conversation with a guy I'd traded flirty text messages with was making my hands shake. I was glad Monica was still holding the rifle.

"First-period English." Jon smiled.

"Speaking of periods, he's in the musical with Monica," Tyler said. I froze. This was not the way I had wanted this conversation between Jon and my dad to go.

Erin responded with a nervous laugh, but Monica rolled her eyes. "Tyler, if you hadn't taken that gun from me already, I would shoot you with it." She whirled toward Dad. "Jon has the best singing voice this high school has seen since . . ."

Her voice trailed off as she tried to think.

"Johnny Cash."

We all turned to look at Jon. He was pointing up in the air toward the speaker near the porch.

"Ain't nobody can sing like Johnny Cash, son." Dad sounded more serious than he was.

"Oh . . . no way, man. He was the master. I mean, I love this song." Jon smiled, and we all heard the music he'd been pointing at. "Ring of Fire" was coming out of the speakers, and Dad raised an eyebrow.

"Where you from again?"

"Just moved down from Chicago."

"And you know Johnny Cash?" Dad was incredulous.

"Know him?" Now it was Jon who couldn't believe it. "He's one of my all-time favorites. Top-five songwriters. Easy."

Dad cocked his head and looked at Jon in a new light. "You shoot as well as you sing?"

Jon smiled. It was dazzling. This kid could charm a bear off a bee's nest. "Not with a gun. Only hunting I ever did up north was with a bow."

Tyler snickered like a sixth grader laughing at a fart joke. "You wear tights with your bow and arrow, Robin Hood?"

"Paula!" Dad called for Mom, who had stepped back into the kitchen with an empty tray and returned with more cookies.

"Yeah, sugar?"

"Grab your bow. Jon here's an archer."

Mom had her bow out of the garage in about two minutes, and I had a knot in my stomach the size of a grapefruit. *Why did I feel like Dad was putting Jon on trial? Why was I so worried whether Dad would like him?* I felt like I was watching *The Hunger Games* live in my own backyard.

As long as I live, I don't think I'll ever forget watching the afternoon sunlight bounce off of Jon's triceps as he pulled that bow back. His T-shirt said PAVEMENT (another band I guess?) and the words "like a rock" flashed into my head as he stood there, focusing, every muscle tensed for just a split second, then: *fwwwwiiiiip/CRASH.*

After he knocked the three remaining cans off the fence, Dad let out an awed, "Holy shit," and handed Jon a Budweiser. Tyler saw this, and we both knew what it meant: Jon was "in" with my dad. It wasn't even a full minute later that Mom called Monica and Erin in to help her set the table, and Tyler said his knee was hurting so he couldn't stay for dinner.

Over Mom's famous fried chicken, Jon filled the whole family in on his move from Chicago, his dad's new position at UAMS, the teaching hospital in town, and he and Dad talked classic country until Mom finally put her foot down and said they could talk more music after Jon helped her dish up dessert. There were homemade brownies with caramel on top, served warm with vanilla ice cream.

Afterward I walked Jon and Monica out to her car. Monica put on her seat belt and rolled down the window. I leaned down, and she kissed me long and hard on the lips. When I looked over at Jon, he was watching with that smirk, and I knew he was thinking about our texts the other night.

As I watched them pull out of the driveway, I sent Jon a message:

```
Nice shooting today.
```

Two seconds later his reply popped up:

```
I've got moves you've never seen. ;)
```

Sunday, September 9

Sitting in church. Here's the genius of keeping this journal: I can write in it while Amy's dad is up there preaching, and everybody just thinks I'm taking notes on the sermon. My mom has a little notebook she brings to church to take notes in and copy down Bible verse references. When I got this out and started writing in it, she just glanced at me and flashed a small smile. She thinks I'm taking interest in church. I feel a little bit guilty for misleading her, but what she doesn't know won't hurt her.

I keep catching myself smiling when I think about Jon's text last night. I feel like I'm walking as close to a campfire as I can with this whole situation—seeing how close I can get to the flame without getting burned. I mean, nothing can actually happen between us. I can't believe I even watched those videos of guys kissing online. I made sure to clear the history in my browser just in case anybody else uses my laptop. It's just not an option for me to be into dudes. As fun as Jon is, I know all we can really have is a good friendship. But maybe it's closer or different from the friendship I have with Tyler. I just never realized I couldn't really be myself around Tyler until Jon showed up. Maybe this is what people mean when they say "bromance." Monica is always saying that about me and Tyler, but I've never sent him flirty text messages before. He'd kick my ass.

Amy is up in the choir loft nodding off. She looks a little hungover from last night. Her dad is wrapping up his sermon now. He's always preaching about how he doesn't even keep booze in their house. He doesn't think it's necessarily wrong to drink, but he thinks it's better to "be controlled by the Holy

Spirit of God" than to be controlled by beer or liquor. He says he doesn't keep any at home because he doesn't want to be tempted by it and possibly put himself in the situation where he might drink too much.

Dad likes Pastor Colbert—he even invited him fishing with us one time—but when this drinking thing comes up, Dad always goes all stiff in the pew. I can feel him tense up. Anyway, Pastor Colbert may not keep any booze in his house, but Amy sure gets her hands on it anyway. I like her just fine, but she's a total party girl.

Sermon's wrapping up now. Going over to Monica's this afternoon so we can study for our English test. How come it's only, like, the third week of school and we've already got tests and quizzes out the ass?

Later . . .

Just got home from Monica's. Girls are so much drama. I mean, we're supposed to be studying for this giant test we have in English, but once we get to her room and pull out our study guides, she leans over and starts making out with me. So that part's awesome and everything, but then when we've been hard-core grinding for like a half hour, I'm chafing in my boxers like crazy. Our shirts are off and she's moaning and groaning, but when I slide a hand down her pants, she sits bolt upright and says, "No! We can't."

I mean, what the hell?

We've been through this a hundred times before, but something about it today just really annoyed me. I grabbed the pillow on her bed and held it over my face and sorta half yelled into it.

She crawled on top of me and ran her hands over my chest. She kept saying, "Babe, you know I'm saving myself."

I rolled my eyes and tried to move her off of me. "You gotta stop getting me all worked up like this if you're just gonna leave me with blue balls every time."

She pushed me back down on the bed and batted her eyelashes. (No, seriously, she actually batted her eyelashes.) "There are *still* plenty of hot things we can do that aren't full-on sex." She unbuttoned my jeans and pulled the zipper down really slowly, still staring me in the eyes. I just let her. If she was gonna bluff, I wasn't gonna call her on it. I'm sick of this weird game of chicken we're playing with sex.

"You want me to keep going?" She was actually sort of purring it like a B-movie star from the seventies.

"Uh, yeah. I do." I was sorta surprised by the way I said it, in this kind of no-nonsense way. It cut through all the BS. She was playing around and I wasn't.

I think she must've gotten the message, because Monica actually pulled down the waistband of my boxers. It felt so good to be out of my jeans after the last half hour that I almost blew when she slid down between my legs and started kissing it. Then she got ambitious and slid it into her mouth, which felt freaking unbelievable for about three seconds before she scraped it with her teeth and I thought she'd bitten it off.

I yelped so loud, she jumped. "What?"

"OUCH! Babe, you gotta watch the teeth."

"Jeez! I was trying to be careful. You're so sensitive—"

"Uh, yeah, I am. Especially there. Christ."

"Well, I'm sorry!" She was fumbling for her shirt. Dammit. We were so close.

"Wait! Babe. It's fine. I was just . . . Here." I grabbed her hands. One I pulled to my mouth and kissed. Then I stuck her finger in my mouth and wrapped my lips over my teeth, sliding them up and down her finger. She instantly stopped squirming around looking for her clothes and stared into my eyes.

She was still straddling me on the bed, and I rocked my hips back and forth underneath her gently as I slowly ran my mouth up and down on her finger. She started to blush, and I could tell this was turning her on. After one more long slurp on her finger, I kissed her fingertip and said, "See? Like that?"

She leaned down and kissed me on the lips, then shook her

head quickly, like she was shaking off a chill, and smirked at me. "We have to study for this test!"

She rolled off of me and grabbed her bra and shirt from the floor. She had both back on before I even sat up.

"What the hell?" I was really pissed.

"What?" She was blinking, big eyes, all innocence, like she had no idea what I was talking about.

"God, I hate it when this happens."

"Oh, don't be such a big baby," she said. "We had our fun. Now we need to study."

I stood up and got everything resituated, then zipped up and grabbed my study guides off the floor.

"Wait—where are you going?"

"Somewhere I can take care of this," I said, pointing at my fly.

"But what about the test?" she said, all pissy.

"Trust me, babe. No way I can focus on a study guide in this condition."

"But I don't want you to just go home."

"Fine." I winked at her. "Let's take care of this here."

"Gross," she said.

For some reason, when she said that, I got so freaking angry. What is it with girls thinking that what happens with dudes and their hard-ons is gross? "Whatever," I said, and walked out of her room and out of her house. She called my name and texted me twice by the time I got back here, but I ignored all of it.

Ten minutes alone in my room with the door locked took care of the pressure. I started off thinking about Monica and sort of saw us in my imagination going at it. I was trying to picture what that would look like, and then it was like the picture in my mind shifted and instead of seeing me and Monica, it was Jon and Monica going at it. I kept seeing Jon's face as he was in action, and instead of making me jealous, for some reason it totally turned me on.

Jesus. What is wrong with me? Jerking off to the idea of my friend getting it on with my girlfriend? If Monica knew about that, she'd never go out with me again.

Monday, September 10
English—First Period

Well, that was a total fail. Crap.

Mrs. Harrison just picked up the tests, and now we're supposed to write in our journals until the bell rings. I should have stayed at Monica's and studied. Way to start off the season. I'm already gonna be in danger of academic probation from the first freaking test. Damn.

Maybe I squeaked by with a D.

Jeez. Who am I kidding?

Tuesday, September 11
Study Hall—Fifth Period

Mrs. Harrison handed back our English tests this morning. I have no idea how she graded all of those essays overnight, but she did it. No D for me. Straight up F. When she dismissed us from class, she walked over to my desk and said, "Let me know when you want to retake the test."

I sort of couldn't believe it.

"Really?" I said.

"No, I'm just standing here teasing you."

Jon heard her say that and tried to stifle a laugh unsuccessfully. She glanced at him and said, "You can have Mr. Statley here help you study."

Jon smiled. "My pleasure."

Mrs. Harrison smiled at Jon. "Excellent. Can you have him ready by Friday?"

"Friday? But I have a game and—"

"Not if you have an F in my class, you don't." Mrs. Harrison smiled. "Jon, I leave the success of our football team in your capable hands."

Jon saluted. "Can you start tonight after my rehearsal and your practice?"

"Sure he can," said Mrs. Harrison. "Clear your schedule. You need to pass this test."

My brain keeps telling me there's a reason to say that I should just study on my own. Something about the idea of hanging out with Jon alone is dangerous—but enticing. Am I excited? Or scared? If I were going to study with Tyler, I wouldn't be either. I'd just be . . . what?

Jesus. Get a grip.

I just need to pass this test so I can play.

Alicia Stevenson left me a message last night. She's bringing the head of recruitment to the game this week. He wants to meet me. I didn't tell anybody yet. I don't want to let my dad down if it doesn't work out.

Plus, Tyler's been really moody. His surgery is scheduled for next week, and he's throwing a preknife party on Friday night after the game. The last thing I want is to ruin his big fun night before weeks of physical therapy by reminding him that I'm talking to scouts when he should be too.

The whole situation totally sucks. I want to be excited about all this great stuff that's happening, but I just feel stressed out by it. It's like I can't be happy about the good things I'm getting because I'm afraid of what everybody else will think.

Later . . .

I thought Jon would be done with rehearsal by the time I hit the showers after practice, but when I got to my truck, there was no sign of him. I walked over to the performing arts center and stepped inside one of the side doors that was propped open. They were just finishing up, and when Mr. London dismissed everybody, Monica came bounding over.

"Want to go get some food?" she asked.

"Can't," I said. "Jon and I are supposed to study tonight so I can retake the English test on Friday."

"I'll come help you study," she said with a grin.

"Absolutely not." Jon had walked up behind me, and I turned around to see him smirking.

"What? Why?" Monica tossed her hair with a huff.

"Because if you're there, this one won't be able to focus on anything but your lips and boobs, and he'll never pass the test."

Monica pleaded and begged all the way out to the parking lot. "I'll wear a big baggy sweatshirt and sit in the corner. You won't even know I'm there."

Jon shook his head and held firm. "The fate of the Hillside Lions hangs on this study session. No girls allowed."

Monica opened her mouth to protest again, but Jon held up a hand. "No! Go flaunt your great and terrible beauty elsewhere. There must be other boys in this town you can torment just for this one evening." He said it in a way that made all of us laugh, and Monica realized further argument was futile. She kissed me on the lips and then got into her car.

"You boys have fun tonight."

Jon's face was a mask of no-nonsense. "Not a chance without you, sugar lips."

Monica dissolved into giggles and drove away.

"How did you do that?" I asked Jon in disbelief.

"Do what?"

"Tell her no and make her happy all at the same time," I said.

He winked at me, and his smirk returned. "Years of practice. Got to stop by my place and grab my study guides. Then I'll head your way. See you at your place?" He jumped behind the wheel of his Jeep without waiting for an answer.

As I started my truck, I couldn't help my smile. Somehow, I am relieved that it's just going to be me and Jon tonight, but I'm not sure why. I thought about it all the way home just now. I put more stuff in my hair and brushed my teeth right when I got here, then ran around my room throwing dirty clothes in the hamper and cleaning up for some reason.

Am I nervous about hanging out with Jon? Jeez. This isn't a freaking date. He just pulled up in the driveway. I have to chill.

Later . . .
It's after eleven p.m. and Jon just left.

That boy kicked my ass with the English. We studied for an hour and a half straight, with him quizzing me from his study guides. He let me get up to pee when my mom brought some Cokes and a plate of brownies up to the room. She wasn't too happy when she found out about the F on the English test, but somehow having Jon here has made her forget all about that. She's totally thrilled that he's helping me out. Even my dad came up to say hi and invite Jon to come along on the hunting trip. I mean, my dad hasn't stepped foot in my bedroom since I was in junior high.

Jon finally pushed them all out. Then we got back to studying for another hour and a half. He made me do a timed essay on the major themes of *Fahrenheit 451*, which I actually read over the summer from the reading list Mrs. Harrison gave us but didn't really understand. Then he made me read the essay out loud and called bullshit when I got to parts where I'd just pulled crap out of my ass.

"Dude. That's a total snow job."

"What?"

"What does that sentence even mean?" He was laughing, and something about the way he gave me criticism didn't make me feel shitty or defensive. It cracked me up too. He was totally right. The whole night, he just patiently explained things in a way that really made sense to me—and kept making me laugh. It didn't feel like a chore, or even like we were studying really. It felt like I was hanging out with a friend, only instead of talking about TV shows and drama at school, we were talking about big ideas—stuff that really matters.

Jon makes me feel like I have good ideas—like I'm not just some big dumb jock—even when I was totally wrong about whatever the hell we were talking about.

When we were going back through the essay together and talking through better ways to express what I was saying, Tracy started blasting that crazy Boison album. I yelled at her to turn it down, and she poked her head in the door.

"Why should I?"

"Because that song *sucks*," I said.

She actually stuck her tongue out at me, and Jon rolled off of the bed where he'd been sitting with his back against the wall and grabbed my guitar off the stand next to my desk.

He started strumming along with the chords in the song, and Tracy's eyes got really big.

"You know Boison songs?" she asked.

"Not really," Jon said. "But I think I've heard this one at the mall, or maybe . . ."

"In your nightmares?" I said.

Jon laughed, but within a minute or so he had figured out the chord progression and Tracy was suddenly enamored. Jon paused, his fingers still on the strings. "Hey, Trace, do me a favor?"

"Sure!" Googly eyes. Pure eighth-grade googly eyes.

"Hit Pause on that iTunes for a sec, would you?"

Tracy disappeared, and the music blessedly stopped. If I'd ever wondered what it would be like to kiss Jon before, now I could hardly stop myself. He started playing the chords again, and I recognized the familiar strains of the Boison song with the line about "the one I've always wanted" that had just been playing. Only . . . there was something different about it.

Jon closed his eyes and noodled around with the notes. There was a slow swing to the song now, a backbeat that he kept tapping out between his foot on the floor and the light slap of his fingers against the wood of the guitar beneath the strings. A cool, syncopated rhythm was happening, and Tracy drifted through the door, mesmerized, sinking onto the bed next to me. This was the song she'd been dancing around her room playing air guitar to for weeks, only somehow . . . it wasn't. In Jon's hands, this dancy pop hook was now a funky down-tempo acoustic ballad.

And then, as he finished playing through the song, Jon closed his eyes and started to sing:

> *You never knew it,*
> *The moment we met*
> *That I'd found a love*
> *I would live to regret*
> *But something in your eyes walked away with my heart.*

Now I'm standing beside you
Holding your hand
Trying like hell
To make you understand
I've fallen for you instead of falling apart.
And
I don't know what happens now
But
I just have to tell you somehow
You're the one I always wanted
You're the one I always wanted
You're the one I always wanted
To love.

Jon's voice floated around the room. It was soft and mellow, full and strong. I realized I was actually hearing the words of this song for the first time, and as I watched Jon sing them, I got a lump in my throat. I'd always hated this song, but when he sang it, it wasn't annoying.

It was beautiful.

As the last notes faded away, Tracy and I just sat there staring in silence while Jon put the guitar back on the stand and then turned around and saw us.

"What?" he asked.

"Dude." It was all I could say.

Tracy jumped up like she was on fire. "That. Was. *Awesome.* Oh my *God*! Play it again! Play it again! I want to record you on my phone."

Jon laughed and checked his watch. "Crap. I gotta jet. It's almost eleven."

"No!" Tracy squealed, running back into the room with her iPhone.

"Seriously," said Jon, grabbing his messenger bag and stuffing his study guides into it. "I'll come back and play it for you again."

Tracy started to follow Jon and me down the stairs. I turned around and shot her a look. "Scram."

She started to argue, but I pointed toward her room, and she got the message that I meant business.

I followed Jon across the front porch and down the stairs. His Jeep was parked in the circle drive behind my truck.

"Where'd you learn how to do that?" I asked him.

"English?" he asked. "I dunno. Just like reading, I guess." He was smirking as he said it.

"No, you jackass. Play the guitar and sing like that."

He shrugged and opened the door, tossing his bag onto the passenger seat. "Just picked it up."

He turned back to face me, and I realized I was standing sort of close to him—like I was going to climb into the Jeep behind him. He was maybe an inch taller than me, and his eyes caught me by surprise. My heart sped up and my knees went soft like they had that day in the hallway looking at the cast list.

He said my name.

I didn't move.

"Hey, man. You okay?"

I realized I hadn't taken a breath. I took one. I nodded. "Yeah . . . I'm . . ."

Jon smiled. Then he raised his right hand and put it on my neck. His fingers were long and cool against my skin. His thumb cupped the square part of my jaw. "I gotta go."

He climbed into the Jeep and closed the door, turning the key and rolling down the window. I could still feel where his hand had rested on my skin, and my brain was a complete flat line.

What was going on?

All I knew was that I didn't want him to go. I wanted him to get out of the Jeep and . . .

And what?

Stay here? Hang out?

I gave my head a quick shake as he popped the parking break and put the Jeep in reverse. "Yeah. Cool. But hey—wait."

He hit the break. "Yeah?"

"We have to study. More. We have to study more. So I

can . . ." My voice trailed off. Why wouldn't my brain form complete sentences?

Jon smiled. "So you can pass the test?"

I nodded.

"Yep. Same time tomorrow?"

I smiled.

He drove away.

Wednesday, September 12
English—Fifth Period

Tyler is in rare form this morning. While I was grabbing my books out of my locker a few minutes ago, Erin was helping Tyler get his, and when she closed his locker, he lost his balance on the crutches and knocked the books out of her hands. Tyler yelled and slammed his fist into the locker.

I reached over to help Erin pick up the books and smiled at Tyler. "It's cool, dude. We got it."

"It's not cool at all," he huffed. Then he turned around and crutched down the hall toward English like there was a cash prize for being the first one at his desk.

"Thanks." Erin was juggling her purse and books, so I grabbed Tyler's and helped her down the hall.

"Is he always this charming, or just when it's this early in the morning?"

Erin smiled with her mouth, but not with her eyes, which suddenly brimmed with tears. "Dang it. I'm sorry."

"Hey—it's okay." I pulled her over to the alcove at the stairs by the door to Mrs. Harrison's room.

"It's not okay," she said, pulling a tissue out of her purse and dabbing under her eyes to keep from smearing her mascara. "Tyler is miserable and he's making everybody else miserable."

"He invited me to that big party on Friday. That'll be fun, right?"

"Don't count on it." Erin blew her nose. Clearly, she had reached her limit.

"You know, you don't have to put up with his crap," I said. "I've been best friends with him longer than anybody, and I know he can be . . ."

"An asshole?"

"I was gonna say 'handful' but . . . yeah. Let's just call this what it is."

When I said this, Erin started laughing, and then I did, too. Monica and Jon raced around the corner just as Erin and I started into class, and the four of us got jammed up in the doorway. Monica made some crazy car crash noise, and Jon laughed, and right as the bell rang, we all slid into our seats.

Mrs. Harrison wasn't in the room yet, and in the general

mayhem, Tyler leaned up in his desk and tapped me on the shoulder.

"Hey, man. You okay?"

"I'm fine." He was smiling, but I could tell something was up. "How was your date last night?"

Monica heard this and whipped around in her seat. "I told you, he's on English test lockdown."

Trevor's eyes widened innocently. "Oh, I know he didn't have a date with you. I was wondering how his date went with Jon."

I rolled my eyes. "We were studying."

"Ooooooh," Tyler said. "A *study* date. Well, that sounds very romantic."

"Jesus. Lay off, would you?"

At that moment, Mrs. Harrison entered the room and told us to take out our journals. Tyler didn't say anything back, but that shit-eating grin he had when I turned around and picked up my pen is still boring into my back. I can barely swallow, and my hand is sweating so badly I might drop my pen.

Just. Keep. Writing.

Out of the corner of my eye, I just saw Jon turn to look at me and glance back at Tyler.

No eye contact. Don't move. Don't look. Don't smile. Just. Keep. Writing.

I can't afford to get on Tyler's bad side right now. He can make life a living hell when he's got a bee up his ass about something.

Study Hall—Fifth Period

Jon texted me at lunch to say he was steering clear of the lunchroom and to see if I wanted to join him in the journalism classroom while he posted some articles on the blog. I texted back that I was eating with Monica.

A few minutes later he wrote:

```
Still on for tonight?
```

I am so tired of feeling scared and worried about something when I have nothing to hide. Still, my fingers paused for longer over the screen than they should have.

```
?? Of course.
```

A couple seconds later Jon replied:

```
Cool. Just didn't know if you were
weirded out by Tyler's comment.
```

Dang. He was good. I was totally weirded out by it, but just the idea that Tyler would be able to control me by embarrassing me made me as angry as I'd been in English this morning. I punched at the screen with my thumbs:

```
Nope. C U after practice.
```

Jon wrote back a single word that made me laugh:

```
*REHEARSAL*
```

Later . . .

Jon had to make good on his promise to sing "The One" again tonight for Tracy so she could make a video of it. It was somehow even better the second time around. Tracy dragged my mom into my room for the performance.

Jon kept his eyes closed as he sang, his voice rich and light—just like last night. Only this time, when he got to the bridge, his eyes opened, and he looked straight in my direction:

> *And*
> *I don't know what happens now*
> *But*
> *I just have to tell you somehow*
> *You're the one I've always wanted. . . .*

The air got really thick in the room. I couldn't catch a

breath. My heart pounded against my rib cage, trying to escape the prison of my chest.

Is Jon singing this . . . to me?

I glanced at my mom, but she was so amazed by Jon singing and playing that she didn't even notice which direction he was looking. When he finished the song, Mom and Tracy clapped wildly, and Tracy rushed off to post the video online.

Mom brought us ice cream sandwiches and told Jon she couldn't wait to see him on stage in *The Music Man*.

Eventually we got down to studying. I tried to put the song out of my head. We were both sprawled across my bed, which is queen-sized, but not so big when two guys and books and study guides are strewn all over it. After an hour of reviewing all the guides and rewriting the essay I worked on last night, Jon put down his pen and sat up.

"You're ready."

"Yeah?"

"Yeah," he said. "You know this stuff now."

"I guess we'll see on Friday."

"Don't wait until Friday. Take the test tomorrow."

"Really?" I asked.

"Totally, man. If you wait, you'll just be freaked out about the game, and your concentration will be blown. Tell

Harrison you want to take it tomorrow in study hall. You'll be fresh."

I nodded. "Cool. Okay, I will."

Jon was gathering up the study guides. He handed them to me. "Hang on to these. Review them one more time before you hit the sack tonight."

"You have to get going?"

Jon checked his watch. "Not yet," he said.

"Good. I want the full story."

His eyes narrowed. "About what?"

"Dude. About Amy. What's going on with you guys?"

Jon rolled his eyes and groaned, flopping down next to me on the bed again. "Nothing." He buried his face in the comforter, but when he looked back up, he had that smirk.

"C'mon, man! Monica is working really hard to get you laid."

"Is she working hard to get *you* laid?" he asked.

"Please. Waiting-for-Marriage Monica?"

"Oh. Oh no." Jon shook his head in mock sadness.

"Oh. Oh yes," I said. "She won't even let me put my hand down her jeans. Should never have broken up with Maria de Soto."

"She your first?" he asked.

"Second," I said. "The first was this girl who lived in my old neighborhood."

Jon nodded. "So, no sex from Monica. She stingy with the blow jobs, too?"

I sort of couldn't believe that he asked me this, and I started laughing. "Dude, she wants to hand those out all the time. It's her go-to instead of having the real deal."

"Well, not a bad consolation prize, right?"

"Wrong! Oh my God, dude. She tries and everything, but the girl is all teeth."

Jon laughed and put both hands over his crotch. "No way! That's the worst."

"No, it isn't," I said. "The worst is that when I try to show her how to do it, she gets all huffy and pouts and puts her clothes back on."

We lay on the bed, laughing like goons for a few seconds.

"Man, that sucks," he said.

"Just for a minute, and then it bites."

We both cracked up again.

"Okay, seriously, Jon. What about you?"

"What about me?"

"Don't play dumb. Have you gotten any action since you came south?"

"Please. Mr. Wiggly's been on bread and water since we packed the U-Haul."

I laughed so hard, I got the hiccups for a second. Jon handed me the bottle of water on my nightstand, and finally I recovered.

"So there *was* somebody in Chicago."

"Maybe," he said. "Don't kiss and tell."

"You're hilarious."

"Likewise. I . . ." His voice trailed off.

"You what?" I asked.

"Nothing. I just . . ." He took a deep breath. "I really like hanging out with you, man. Thanks for being my friend."

"Phffff. Whatevs. You're the one doing *me* a favor. Seriously. You're gonna help me pass English, keep my scholarship a possibility. Plus you can charm the pants off Monica, my mom, and my freaking sister, and all you have to do is sing. Jesus. You're magic."

Jon blushed and looked down at his hands. "Well, I really like you. You're my first real friend here."

I smiled. "Jesus. I can't believe neither one of us is getting laid."

Jon shrugged. "Seriously. It's not like we're ugly. And you're the freaking quarterback."

"We're gonna change this," I said. "Whatcha doing Friday after the game?"

"No plans."

"Cool. You and Amy are gonna double with me and Monica to Tyler's party."

"You sure that's a good idea?" Jon looked worried.

"What do you mean?" I asked.

"You know. Tyler doesn't seem to be a big fan of mine."

"Screw him," I said. "He's just being a dick because of his knee. Besides, he'll be so wasted on Friday night he won't know who's there anyway."

Jon nodded slowly. "I guess, if you think it'll be cool."

"Guess? I know it'll be cool. Trust me. I'm a quarterback. We're natural-born leaders."

The smirk crept back onto his face. "I'd follow you anywhere."

Friday, September 14
English—First Period

Told Harrison I wanted to take the test yesterday. I think she was surprised, but I told her I was ready, so I sat in the back of her junior class during fifth period when I'm usually in study hall.

This morning she had it graded and waiting for me when I walked by the lectern on the way to my desk.

I got a B.

That's the best grade I've ever gotten in English.

Ever.

And the test didn't even feel hard. I knew that stuff—I actually knew it. I just remembered what Jon and I had talked about and even the essay wasn't too bad.

Jon is such a good guy. He's the kind of friend I didn't know

I wanted. I guess when all you have to compare friendship to is Tyler, you don't really know what you're missing.

Not to get all mushy and weird, but Jon really seems to care for me. And not just me, but he seems to care for people in general. He doesn't put people down and run around saying crass, stupid shit.

I've never really had a friend like him before.

Can't wait to celebrate this with him. I flashed him the test right as I sat down, and he gave me a high five across the aisle.

Of course, then Tyler made stupid kissing noises in my ear for the first five minutes of class, but who cares? Fuck him. This is a big deal for me. I'm gonna show Jon a good time tonight.

I don't give a shit what Tyler thinks.

Saturday, September 15

Jon was gone already this morning when I woke up. I can't believe I didn't hear him leave. I guess I was drunker than I thought I was last night. My head feels like somebody parked a Land Rover on it.

The weird part is that I feel sort of . . . I dunno. Disappointed? Is disappointed the right word? The right idea? I mean, that's what I feel. As soon as I opened my eyes and looked over to the other side of the sectional, I saw that the blanket Jon had used and the shorts of mine he'd borrowed last night were folded up neatly. I knew he was gone then, and I felt totally bummed out.

Is that normal?

Jesus. Nothing about this is normal. I rolled off my side of couch onto the floor and just lay there for a minute with my face pressed into the carpet. Then I pushed myself up and was so sore—which was when I remembered that Jon and I had lifted weights last night, drunk as hell. It all came rushing back to me, and I started laughing, which made my head hurt even worse.

I grabbed the shorts Jon wore last night and the comforter I pulled off my bed for him and went to get some Advil and a bottle of water. Nobody else is awake yet, so I came up to my room and was gonna get back in bed, but I just knew that between my head hurting from the Maker's last night and this weird sad feeling in my stomach, I wouldn't be able to go back to sleep. I honestly don't know which thing feels worse.

That's why I want to write about it, I guess. Seems like I've been doing that a lot lately.

Anyway, before I started writing, I sent Jon a text:

```
Dude. U left. U OK?
```

Now I'm checking my phone every twenty seconds like a crackhead to see if he's written back. Nothing yet. Sometimes

I think it's better to just not text people at all. The only thing that's worse than not getting a text from someone first is sending *them* a text and then having them not respond. It's excruciating. Like my headache.

Screw it. As long as I'm up and waiting on a text message, I might as well write about last night—which was mostly fun, with a few moments of complete bullshit thrown in.

The fun part started with winning the game. Almost every pass I threw connected. The guys were just on fire yesterday. Tracker could catch anything I tossed him. He was sprinting, leaping, and scrambling to get open. He was a pass magnet. And Watters was like magic. Anytime I couldn't find Tracker, Mike would just pop up and I'd zip it to him, low and tight. At halftime, I'd already passed for 260 yards, including three touchdowns, and we were up twenty-one to three.

Coach was actually smiling.

Coach. Never. Smiles.

Second half was more of the same. I broke the school record for passing yards in a single game—which I didn't actually know until I came out of the locker room and Roger Jackson asked me how it felt. I just blinked at him and smiled. He badgered me with questions for his column in the paper as Alicia Stevenson introduced me to the lead recruiter for OU and almost got knocked off her heels by the recruiter from

University of Arkansas, this tall bald guy with a goatee who looks like he could be a professional wrestler. He charged right up and stepped into the circle and interrupted Alicia, who was interrupting Roger:

"Bill Harris. U of A. We can make you a star. I've got a full ride with your name on it and a guarantee you'll start as a sophomore."

I had seen this guy before.

I had heard these words before.

Bill Harris had made this same offer to Tyler after practice, two weeks before school started. I remember, because I was standing right there when he charged up and introduced himself.

This time, he was saying these words to me, and right as he said them, I saw Tyler, Erin, Monica, Jon, and Amy standing behind him. They'd all come over to congratulate me. We were headed to the party at Tyler's. The look on Tyler's face when Bill Harris said these words told me that our plans would probably change.

"What the hell?"

Tyler's voice was loud, angry, and carried halfway across the field. Bill Harris jumped when he heard it and spun around to see Tyler on his crutches, red-faced and pissed as all hell.

Bill held up both hands. "Take it easy, son. I'm sorry about your injury, but—"

"Take it *easy*? You asshole. You just gave my best friend *my scholarship offer*. Get the hell out of my face." Tyler was spitting, he was yelling so hard. Erin put a tentative hand on his arm, but he shook it off.

Bill backed away but shoved a card into my hands. "I'll be in touch," he whispered as he retreated toward the parking lot.

"Oh, you'll be in touch, will you? You fucker!" Tyler's voice echoed across the emptying stadium and stands. Heads turned, eyes widened. This was quickly becoming what my mom would call a "scene."

The look in Tyler's eyes was crazy. Alicia and the head honcho from OU also mumbled good-byes to me and fled toward their cars.

"And who the hell are *you*?" Tyler had taken to swinging steps up to Roger Jackson, who was busy scribbling down the scene in a tiny memo pad. "You that pansy-ass reporter from the *Gazette*? Here's something to report for your column. Hillside High's new superstar here has something besides a great arm. He's a fairy with the hots for the new kid."

He spun to face me. "You fucking traitor. Just gonna take everything that's mine, huh? You can take your scholarship and shove it up your ass. And don't come to my party tonight. You can just have fun hanging out with your new boyfriend."

"Dude. You need to chill out." Jon's voice was quiet, but firm.

All the adults had run away from the heat of Tyler's rage, but not Jon. When Tyler heard this, he lost his shit. He yelled at the top of his lungs and swung his right crutch at Jon's head. It happened so fast, but Jon caught the rubber stopper in his left hand, and Tyler fell backward, thrown off balance. I grabbed for him as he headed toward the ground and was able to break his fall a bit. We both ended up on the pavement.

Jon leaned over and offered Tyler his hand. Tyler snorted and spit on Jon's palm, then unleashed every name in the book:

Fairy, fag, homo, fudge packer, butt pirate . . .

The anger coursed through me like a power surge blowing a lightbulb. I leaped to my feet and tried to fling myself at Tyler. I wanted to stop the sounds coming out of his mouth any way I could. If that was a fist through his face, so be it. As I tried to get between him and Jon, Jon put a hand on my chest and held me back.

"I got this," he said. There was something so strong and sure in Jon's voice that I looked into his eyes, away from Tyler. I saw something there I'd always wanted to see in Tyler's eyes but never had: certainty.

No matter how tight Tyler and I had gotten, or how many hours we spent together hanging out on the football field or hunting or playing video games or just listening to music and driving around in my truck, I realized in this moment that I'd

116

always been afraid: afraid of his judgment of everything and everyone, afraid I wasn't cool enough, afraid that he would turn on me, afraid that any moment, he would learn my secret and he would snap, afraid that I would one day become the unseen enemy he was always fighting.

Now that seemed to be happening, and as one of my worst fears became a reality, there was Jon, stepping in between us, telling me with a single look that in just a few weeks, we'd developed a friendship worth *not* fighting for, that I would never have to worry about him turning on me. That he would be there for me in a way Tyler had never been. The look in Jon's eyes stirred something inside me, and for the first time I realized I could make a choice about my friendships. I could choose to feel something more important than popular. I could choose to feel peaceful.

Trying to keep this friendship with Tyler had been so frustrating and painful, and I'd always felt racked with the fear that if I didn't do it just right, this very thing would happen. What had all that work and effort and trust and trying been for if it made me feel miserable?

It only took a second for these thoughts to flash through my head, and all at once, I didn't want to brain Tyler anymore. He was still hurling insults at us from the ground, but I just felt sorry for him.

Jon leaned in and whispered, "Stay cool, man. There's a reporter here. Let's get him up."

Tyler fought us, but I took Jon's lead, and we got him back on his feet and got his crutches under his arms. He screamed at us the whole time. "Get your faggoty fingers off me!"

Once he was standing, Jon gave me a quick nod. "Let's get out of here." He said it to the whole group. Monica and Amy each had an arm around Erin, who was crying on the curb. The girls tried to get Erin to come with us, but she shook her head. "I have to get him home."

Tyler yelled put-downs and curses after us all the way to the parking lot. He was still shouting as we agreed to meet at my place and piled into our cars. I'd always been grateful to be on Tyler's good side and wondered what it was like for people who weren't.

After last night, I don't have to wonder anymore. It's pretty terrible.

At my place, Dad had gotten started celebrating at halftime with a six-pack he'd stashed in his truck, and Mom had driven him home right after the last play. He'd gone straight for the fridge and was pretty tanked when we all walked in. He was hooting and hollering and giving high fives. I steered us all out the back door, and we walked through the trees by iPhone light, down the trail to the running path along the river that leads to the bridge over the dam.

Jon pulled a flask of Maker's Mark out of his back pocket and passed it around.

"Thanks a lot," I said.

"For what?" Jon asked.

"Just . . . reminding me to keep my cool."

Monica rolled her eyes. "God, Tyler is such a dick."

Jon shrugged. "This has to be hard on him."

"He's not losing his leg. He's just missing the season," Amy said. "It's not the end of the world."

"It might feel like it to him, though," I said.

Monica threw her hands up in the air. "Please. When he got named quarterback, you didn't run around crying and pouting— or being an asshole to everybody."

She had a point.

"Sorry he called you both all those names." Amy said this to Jon, who raised the flask in a toast and took a swig.

Monica reached over and grabbed it from him with a laugh. "Enough about Tyler. Jesus. We have a B on an English test, a broken record, and three wins this season to celebrate."

Jon hooted and gave Monica a high five, and the two of them talked about me getting the offer from University of Arkansas. Monica was the most excited about that. She's been planning to go to U of A since she was a little girl. Her mom and dad met there, and she jumped up and down in her cheerleading uniform on the bridge.

"It's amazing! Now we'll go to the same college, and I'll be dating a U of A quarterback!"

Jon shot me a glance, but I stayed quiet and smiled. There was no way I was going to the same school that Tyler had hoped to go to. He might still end up there on scholarship if his knee healed up and he was in shape enough to do a walk-on practice in the spring. After tonight, I wanted to get as far away from Tyler during college as possible. But for now, I let Monica have her vision of going to the same place for college.

"Not to bring everybody down," said Amy, "but what are things going to be like on Monday with Tyler? It's not like we aren't going to see him again."

"It'll blow over," I said. Jon looked unconvinced. Monica looked pissed at the thought of it. "It will," I said. "He'll be out next week anyway. His surgery is on Monday morning, and I'll go see him once he gets home. He won't stay mad."

"Why?" Monica asked.

"Why what?" I frowned.

"Why are you going to go see him?

"He's my . . . friend." I almost said "best" friend, but something stopped me. It dawned on me that maybe best friends didn't treat each other the way Tyler had treated me—even when they were angry at each other.

"That's really big of you," said Jon. "Proud of you, man." He

120

held out the flask, and we passed it around the circle one more time.

Monica was a little tipsy from her three swallows of Maker's Mark, and she always gets kissy when she's buzzed. She pulled me down the running path off the bridge to a picnic table under a big elm tree in the grass along the river. She pushed me down onto the bench, my back against the edge of the table, and she straddled me, kissing me with soft, sweet lips that smelled like lip gloss and bourbon.

Her short cheerleading skirt didn't cover much and before long she was grinding against the fly of my jeans with the slick fabric of her Under Armour. I closed my eyes and let the warmth of the bourbon coursing through me take over, but as I felt her lips against mine and her hips against mine, I heard Amy's laugh float over the water down from the bridge, and I had to resist the urge to pull away and look.

What did Jon say? Are they making out too?

I kept my eyes closed, and my hands ran down Monica's back, then pushed her hips even tighter down on my lap. I saw a flash of Jon kissing Amy in my imagination. His eyes were closed, and his arms were wrapped around her, one hand on the back of her head.

"Whoa . . . hang on, mister." Monica came up for air. "Whew! That was intense."

My heart was racing, and I was short of breath. Why was

she always stopping when it got good? I tried to lean in to kiss her again, but she swung a leg out of the picnic table and slid off my lap. She tossed her hair and stood up, then leaned over and pecked me on the lips.

"Where are you going?" I asked with a smile. "Get back here."

"We have to go," she said.

"What? Why? Now? We just got here." She was already headed back toward the bridge. I followed her.

"I have rehearsal tomorrow at nine a.m. sharp. It's almost midnight." She started giggling.

"What's so funny?"

She turned and threw both arms around my neck with a big smile. "I'm too tipsy to keep making out. If I did, I might not want to stop."

"That's fine with me," I whispered, and tried to kiss her again. She pulled away and called for Amy, who jumped up with Jon and came walking down the running path from the bridge to meet us.

When we got back to my place, I tried to convince the girls to come in, but Monica wouldn't hear of it. Amy was too looped from the bourbon to drive home. I parked Amy's car on the street and she climbed in with Monica, who gave Jon strict instructions not to be late.

That's probably why he had to leave so early. It's barely nine thirty now. He must've gone home to shower and change. I wonder if he's half as hungover as I am.

We polished off the Maker's Mark after the girls left, and I was feeling no pain, but Jon didn't seem too screwed up, just really smiley. He has such a great smile that it makes me smile just to think about it. I guess you'd call that infectious.

Anyway, we were sitting on the front porch when I drank the last of the bourbon and handed the flask back to him.

"And . . . good night." He screwed the top back on the silver flask.

"Are you leaving?" I asked.

"You want me to?" Did I mention his smile?

My instinct was to yell, *Hell NO!* Something inside me— some quiet fear—told me to play it cool. I shrugged. "You can crash here if you want."

Jon stood up and stretched. His shirt said IMPERIAL TEEN and had a picture of an old-fashioned electric fan on it—the kind with the three blades behind a metal cage. I tried like hell to keep my eyes on the graphic on the shirt instead of the hem that I knew was riding up and showing off his abs again. *Is he going to leave?*

He turned toward me on the stairs and said, "Okay, well . . . yeah. If it's no trouble, I think I'll crash here. Just gonna text my mom."

He pulled out his phone, and the glow of the screen briefly lit up his face as he tapped out a message. I thought about the image of him kissing Amy that had flashed through my mind earlier and stared at his lips in the cool blue light from his phone.

We headed inside. "Wanna watch some TV or something?" I asked.

"Sure . . . or something."

These words shot down my spine and made my stomach do somersaults. *What did he mean?* I forced myself not to turn around and just led the way downstairs to the rec room where our media center is. I flipped on the TV and tossed Jon the remote.

"We can sleep down here," I said, pointing to the massive sectional. It made a big L in the room, and there was plenty of room for one of us on each of the sides. "My bed's a little . . . small."

"A queen." Something about the way he said this—it was like he was making a joke, but I wasn't sure. And if he was making a joke, I didn't get it. He smiled and let me off the hook. "This is perfect. You mind if I borrow some shorts to sleep in?"

I just blinked at him. Maybe the booze was making me stupid.

"You know, like, just some gym shorts?" He tried to help me out.

"Oh!" I laughed. "Sure, no sweat. Be right back." I ran upstairs and changed out of my jeans into workout shorts and grabbed an extra pair for Jon. I got a couple sheets and blankets from the hall closet and the pillows off my bed, then headed back downstairs.

"There's a bathroom right there," I said, tossing Jon the shorts and pointing. I started to spread the sheets out on both sides of the couch and tossed a blanket and pillow on top of both.

"It's cool," he said. He kicked off his sneakers and shucked off his jeans right there. He was so casual and slow about it, like he didn't care if I looked or not. He was wearing these really cool boxer briefs—gray with bright neon-green stripes and waistband. My eyes wandered across the bulge in the front, and I immediately felt my cheeks go red. I spun back around and started tucking the sheet in on my side of the sectional. I did this with such intense focus that you'd have thought my entire goal in life was to secure this freaking sheet under the cushions. *Don't look Don't look Don't look Don't look* was pounding in my ears.

I turned back around when I heard Jon toss his jeans onto the couch. I was just in time to see him lift the hem of his T-shirt and pull it off over his head. This time, I couldn't move. His torso was so lean and ripped, you could see every single muscle.

"Dude!" I just started laughing.

"What?" He turned around, wide-eyed, like he was completely oblivious.

"You're just . . . totally cut up. Damn. Your six-pack is an eight-pack."

He smirked and raised an eyebrow. "Butterfly, man. It's not just you meatheads packing on the muscle. The swim boys will give you a run for your money."

Maybe it was the bourbon, or the challenge, or both. I pulled off my T-shirt from the neck and dropped it on the carpet, then grabbed a couple of forty-pound dumbbells from the weight rack in the far corner next to the pool table. "Let's do this."

Jon started laughing. "Bring it."

I started with iron crosses, and I couldn't believe it: Jon matched me set for set, pound for pound, until we were both beet red, sweating and grunting like idiots. Finally I collapsed on the floor, and he leaned over me, smirking.

"Had enough?"

We both laughed, but there was something about the way he said that; it made me wonder for a second what he was talking about. I grabbed a couple of waters from the fridge under the bar and tossed him one. I was breathing pretty hard.

"You're panting like you were earlier tonight with

Monica." Jon settled in on the sectional and winked.

"Dammit. That girl. Always getting me worked up and then leaving me high and dry."

Jon nodded. "She's such a prick tease."

"Yes! That's exactly what she is. What about you? How'd it go with Amy?"

"Don't kiss and tell."

"Oh, c'mon," I said. "Gimme a break. You had the perfect chance to put the moves on her."

"Let's just say you're not the only one with blue balls."

I tried to pry some details out of him, but he was solid as a rock. He wouldn't even give me a hint. At some point we both drifted off to sleep, and when I saw that he wasn't here this morning, I had this weird wave of disappointment flood over me. I just felt really bummed.

My phone just chimed. It was Jon:

```
Dancing with a hangover is hell. =P
```

I wrote back:

```
Had fun last night.
```

His response just flashed up:

Me 2. Call u l8r.

And just like that, I feel 100 percent better. Just because he texted me. This is ridiculous. I am losing my shit over this guy.

I'm scamming on him in his boxer briefs and letting my eyes wander all over his muscles. I'm seeing him in my head when I'm making out with my girlfriend. This whole thing is supposed to be a secret, and for the first time in my life—since I was a little kid in second grade and tried to hold hands with Bobby Lamont in the carpool—I am allowing myself to actually entertain the idea that I like a guy.

Not just like.

That I am turned on by this guy.

There. I wrote it. See? That wasn't so hard.

But what if somebody were to see that? What if somebody actually knew? What if my dad knew? He'd lose his shit. I cannot let anybody find out about this. I have to keep this to myself. I have to keep my head in the game, as Coach would say. It's bad enough that Tyler is being a douche bag.

I can't deal with this right now. I have to get out of school. I have to nail down a scholarship. I have get to college. All that stuff could fall apart on me if I'm not careful.

Still, I'm glad Jon is gonna call me later.

There's nothing wrong with us being friends.

Sunday, September 16

Back in church.

Pastor Colbert is going at it today. He started talking about the election in November and how our nation is going down the "moral sewer." He says God is angry at our country for legalizing abortion and giving homosexual people rights. He's all red in the face, talking about the agenda that homosexuals are trying to push on young people.

When he said this, I got scared and angry at the same time. I'm a young person. No homosexual has ever tried to push an agenda on me. What does that even mean? What would that look like? This is freaking crazy that he's preaching this sermon today. It's like he can read my mind. Or my journal. I mean, what if I'm a gay person? I don't want to push an agenda on anybody else. What is he talking about?

Jeez. Pastor Colbert just said that homosexuals are "an abomination," and my dad and, like, twenty other men in the congregation shouted out "AMEN!" really loudly. I can feel myself blushing. I want to get up and go to the bathroom, or just get out of this room somehow, but then everybody would see me leave. Would they think it's because I'm afraid that I'm gay? Do they think I'm gay already?

My hand is shaking while I write this. All I can think about is talking to Jon last night. When he called, I was getting ready for bed. We talked for like twenty minutes about his day and rehearsals for the musical and how much fun we had hanging last night. I kept picturing him the night before and how he looked in those boxer briefs. (Why can't I get that image out of my head?) I got totally turned on while I was talking to him.

I want to look up from this notebook, but every time I do, I see my mom nodding at Pastor Colbert, and I wonder if she and Dad can tell what I've been writing in this notebook. Is this a sign from God? What if he's not angry at the whole country? What if he's just angry at me?

What if everybody knows I'm gay? What if Mom is nodding and Dad is saying "Amen" because they want me to know that I'd better not even think about being a homo?

My hand is shaking, and I feel like I'm gonna throw up. I want to run out of this building and never come back.

Later . . .

On my way out of church, Monica reminded me that I'm supposed to come over for dinner. That is *exactly* what I need to do. I am going to her house for dinner, and then I'm going to make out with her like crazy. Maybe we can go for a drive out to Pinnacle Mountain and climb into the back of my truck like we did last summer. Jon is a nice guy and everything, but it's just not an option for me.

There are a couple kids at school who have announced that they're lesbian or gay. One sophomore says he's "bisexual." They get picked on all the time, even though the teachers are supposed to be on the lookout for bullies. Those kids don't have many friends. They don't have any power.

The gay people I've seen on TV are all lawyers or interior designers or artists. A lot of times the actors who play them are straight—or at least claim to be. I've seen only one or two gay characters who actually like sports or are into the things that I'm into. Most of the time they're really funny or really dramatic or really fashionable or superbitchy. Sometimes they go on dates or have a "partner." Every once in a while they might kiss, but it's never for very long, or like they're really into it—at least not on the shows I've seen. I mean, I'm usually at practice or doing homework, and it's not like my dad is going to sit and watch "fags" on TV, so usually the second any story line takes that turn, he flips the channel to ESPN.

And who are these people that Pastor Colbert was talking about? These gays with the agenda? I mean, that's not me either.

None of these people are who I am.

Maybe I'm not really gay. Maybe I just need to focus on girls. Maybe I just need to find a girl who will freaking sleep with me.

Monica may not do that, but she'll at least make out with me and maybe even give me a blow job. At least that's a start.

Later . . .

Okay, if there really is a capital-G "God," he's screwing around with me.

I get to Monica's for dinner. Usually it's just me, Monica, and her mom when I go over there for dinner. Her mom usually has a little too much wine and talks about what a "sweet boy" I am and insists that I call her "Barbara" instead of Ms. Nichols. If she gets to that point with the wine drinking, she'll also tell us how she wishes she had married somebody half as nice as me instead of Monica's dad, who took off with his secretary when Monica was six. Typically, this whole line of conversation makes me a little uncomfortable, but she's generally a really nice lady. Plus, when I come to dinner, she always makes steaks. I'm a sucker for a good steak.

Anyway, so I'm walking up to the front door of Monica's house when this dude swings open the door and steps out onto the porch. He's shorter than me and has dark hair like Monica's. He's wearing an Arkansas Travelers T-shirt and jeans with low-top Chuck Taylor tennis shoes. The T-shirt shows off his arms and chest, and he stops when he sees me on the stairs.

"Oh—hey. Dang. Monica wasn't kidding about you."

I smile, but I'm confused. "Hey, I'm—"

"Oh, I know all about who you are." He laughs and holds out a hand. "Sorry. I'm Brent. Barbara's brother. Headed out to get the wine I left in the car. Gimme a hand?"

Monica had mentioned her uncle Brent before, but I'd never met him. I thought she'd said he lived in Memphis and traveled a lot for work. I guess I'd pictured some old guy with a beer belly and a goatee. Not . . . well, this guy who looked like he hit the gym a lot.

Anyway, we get inside, and Barbara reintroduces us while she opens the wine and finishes cooking the steaks. Monica kisses me, and I help her set the table. The whole time, Brent is telling me stories about the guys Monica's mom used to date when she was in high school. Brent is three years younger than Barbara, so he was a freshman when she was a senior, and his memories about the guys were cracking me and Monica up.

When we sit down to eat, Brent is telling us about this guy Barbara used to date when she was a senior who would give him a joint if Brent would let him climb in the bedroom window at night so he could sneak into Barbara's room.

Monica was shocked. "Mom!"

Barbara sighed. "Let's just say I didn't make the best choices as a high school student. You've done much better than I have, Monica." She winked at me, and I blushed.

"I'll say," said Brent. "Monica tells me you're breaking records on the football field."

"Got lucky," I said.

"Whatever, man. Nobody is that lucky. That's hard work and sheer talent."

"Thanks," I said. I am still not used to taking compliments. I tried to change the subject. "You a Travelers fan?" I asked, pointing at Brent's T-shirt.

"Sorta," he said. "This guy I was seeing was. We drove over for a bunch of games this summer."

My brain sort of shut down when he said "guy I was seeing." I must've looked like an idiot, because I just stared at him. *Brent is . . . gay?*

Barbara didn't miss a beat. She laughed and poured some more wine. "Talk about poor choices."

Brent shook his head. "Jesus. What was I thinking? I mean, I thought this guy was the one: loved baseball as much as I do, hot as hell."

Monica piped up, "Yeah, he was gorgeous."

I felt like I'd been transported to Mars. "This was your ex-boyfriend?" I asked.

Brent laughed. "Well, 'boyfriend' might be a strong term for it. We were dating."

Barbara snorted. "Brent saved *his* poor choices in men for adulthood."

"I liked him," Monica said. She turned to me. "Brent has had a run of bad luck."

"It's not so easy," he protested. "I just want to find somebody who is in good shape and actually has a brain. It's a plus if he's into sports a little. I just can't watch *The Real Housewives* twenty-four-seven."

I couldn't believe it. I almost expected to be on one of those hidden camera shows. It was just what I'd been writing about in this journal this afternoon. I mean, here was a gay guy who was . . . like me. Into sports, seems pretty normal.

"What do you do for a living?" I asked Brent.

"Pharmaceutical rep. Pays the bills. Lots of vacation time when I want it. Was able to get to Florida this year and catch some preseason baseball during spring training."

Brent was exactly the opposite of the gay guys I'd seen on TV. I mean, he was handsome and funny, but not in a bitchy way. He was real, and nice. He didn't seem like he was out to corrupt anybody or push his ideas on others.

"So, what did you guys do today?" Brent directed the question at Monica.

"Well, we went to church this morning," she said.

"And how was that?" Brent raised an eyebrow when he asked.

"Weird." I just blurted it out. I didn't mean to, but I said it before I thought about it. Everybody looked at me, and Barbara laughed.

"Yeah, that sermon was a little over-the-top for my tastes." She sighed.

"Fire and brimstone?" Brent asked.

"No, more election-year politics," Barbara said. "We veered into 'gay agenda' territory."

Brent rolled his eyes. "Jesus, Barb. Why are you dragging my niece to a place like that?"

"Please, Brent. She's dragging me."

"It's just that all my friends go there. Usually it's pretty good."

"What was weird about it for you?" Brent asked me.

I felt my cheeks flush as everybody waited for me to answer. I took a drink of iced tea to stall for time. "I don't know," I said. "I just feel like . . . well, this morning, it got all judgmental. I mean, isn't God supposed to be about love?"

"You'd think," Brent said, helping himself to more mashed potatoes.

Barbara sighed again. "Some Sundays I swear that preacher is trying to make Episcopalians out of all of us."

"Well, let me tell you about my homosexual agenda," Brent said. "First, I want to mandate that all gay pride parades end at a baseball game. There should be free draft beer for anybody who wants one. We'll make the lesbians pitch, and we'll have the musical theater boys do a big number on the pitcher's mound during the seventh-inning stretch."

This cracked me and Monica up, and as we all sat there laughing, this big wave of relief swept over me. Brent was a guy I identified with. He was somebody I'd like to be friends with. He was somebody I could see myself being like in my thirties. I'd never met anybody quite like him who was so . . . at ease in his own skin.

Monica wanted to study for a history quiz we have tomorrow, and of course we wound up making out for a little while in her room after dinner, but the urgency to get her into the car and prove something to myself was gone. I left to come home before she got me too worked up and left me hanging again.

On the way out, Brent shook my hand and told me he was back in town at the end of next week for some meetings.

"Maybe I'll stop by and catch the game next Friday," he said. "Wanna see you in action with that magic passing arm."

"Sure thing," I said. "Tell Monica if you can make it."

Barbara gave me a hug, and Monica walked me out to the car.

"You never told me your uncle is gay," I said.

"I don't know. I guess I just don't think of him as 'gay,'" she said. "I just think of him as Uncle Brent."

Something about that stuck with me as I drove home. Maybe I'm making way too much of this whole thing. Maybe I should stop worrying so much about being gay or being straight and just be me.

Tyler had left me a voice mail during dinner at Monica's. He said he was sorry about the whole scene on Friday night and asked me to call him back. When I did, he apologized again.

"It was really lame," I said.

"Yeah, man, I know." He was squirming on the other end of the phone. "I just . . . I guess I'm just really jealous."

"Of what? You're going to get back in shape, and this spring you'll still be able to go do a walk-on at U of A. They'll still give you a scholarship."

"I know."

There was silence for a minute. I wasn't sure how to bring it up, so I just forged ahead.

"You gotta chill out about Jon," I said.

Tyler didn't say anything.

"You still there?" I asked.

"Yeah."

"He's a good guy."

"Whatever," he said.

"No, Tyler, not whatever. Jon is a good guy. You've gotta give him a chance."

"I just . . ." Tyler's voice trailed off.

"You just what?" I asked.

"I just liked it when it was you and me."

"Well, then act that way, man. Stop calling me names and

138

being a tool. I'm really sorry that you got hurt. You're my best friend. I didn't want that to happen. But it's not my fault, and it sure as hell isn't Jon's."

We talked about the schedule for his surgery, and I told him I'd text him tomorrow night to see how he was doing. We made plans that I'd come by on Tuesday after class if he was feeling okay.

I can't believe how much better I feel after tonight. Still, I have this little knot in the pit of my stomach every time I think about Pastor Colbert's sermon this morning. It's not the sermon, really. It's the sight of Mom nodding and the sound of Dad's voice shouting, "Amen."

I wonder how Brent figured out he wasn't an "abomination."

Monday, September 17
English—First Period

Mrs. Harrison put a topic on the board this morning: WHAT YOU SEE WHEN YOU CLOSE YOUR EYES.

She had all of us close our eyes for fifteen seconds. Now we're supposed to write about what we saw.

The last thing I saw before I closed my eyes was Jon's triceps pressing against the sleeve of his T-shirt across the aisle, one desk up. Today his T-shirt says MOUNTAIN GOATS, and of course, that made me think of his IMPERIAL TEEN T-shirt from Friday night, and *that* made me think of him peeling that shirt off in our rec room. All I can see is him grabbing the hem of that shirt and pulling it up, up, up, revealing the bright green waistband of those boxer briefs he was wearing. I can see him undoing the buckle on his belt and sliding his jeans off and every ripple in his abs, his chest, his shoulders as wide as a house from swim practice.

My heart is pounding right now as I think about it. I can barely catch a breath.

I just glanced up at Jon, and it was almost like he *knew*. He turned around and winked at me across the aisle. Now I really can't breathe. I just have to keep my hand moving across this page until time is up. I can't think too much about this. I can't let myself fall into this excitement and this fear. It feels too deep and too difficult when I think about it.

Just be me.

Just be me.

Just be me.

Jesus. Thank God Tyler isn't here today. I feel like a crazy person.

Wednesday, September 19
English—First Period

Last night after practice, I was heading to my car when I saw that the side exit doors of the theater building were propped open way across the parking lot, and I heard music coming through them. I was tired, but I wondered who was singing, so I tossed my bag into my truck and walked over. I poked my head into the back door, farthest from the stage.

The music stopped right as I walked in. The whole theater was dark except for the stage lights, which were on full blast, and it looked like the entire cast was in this number. Mr. London jumped up onto the stage and talked to Jon about something, pointing and telling him to step up on this box in the middle of the stage on a certain word.

"That'll be the big statue in the town square once the set is done," he explained.

"Got it." Jon nodded.

Mr. London jumped back down off the stage and turned to the music teacher, Miss Lee, who raised her arms and beat out a four count. The whole band, including a piano, jumped to life, and as the music began, Jon strode to the center of the stage like he owned the place.

He started half talking/half singing at the rest of the cast, who were all leaning in toward him with their hands on their knees, bouncing along with the music. It was sort of like an old-fashioned rap, only there was no slang, and it was funny.

Jon's voice was strong and clear, and he was saying all these words really fast, but really clearly and in rhythm to this group of townspeople. He was warning them about their kids frittering away their days shooting pool at the town pool hall and how there was "Trouble, right here in River City." He ran around the stage, whipping the crowd into a frenzy of singing, all raising their hands and singing harmonies on the word "trouble" each time Jon said it.

As the song ended, Jon jumped up onto the box Mr. London had pointed out and shouted "Trouble with a capital T, that rhymes with P, which stands for POOL!" I actually laughed out loud, and Mr. London turned around and stared into the darkness, and I panicked and ducked out the side door, but not before I saw a big grin spread over Jon's face.

By the time I got home, I had a text from Jon:

Who u lurkin' at? LOL

Me:

#caught

Jon:

I'd know that laugh anywhere.

Me:

```
u r amazing up there!!
```

Jon:

```
thanx. call u 18r. =)
```

I was at Tyler's place when Jon called. Tyler had texted me and said he was feeling better if I wanted to stop by. He was all doped up on pain meds, but it was good to see him, and he smiled this big stoned smile.

"You oughta try knee surgery sometime, man," he slurred. "The drugs rock."

His eyes were glassy, and he got tired pretty quickly, but it was good to see him. I helped his mom change the ice in this cooler that runs cold water through a pack around his knee to help keep the swelling down. It's the most high-tech ice pack I've ever seen.

Is it bad that I like Tyler better on pills? He's way more chill.

Friday, September 21
English—First Period

I'm nervous. I'm not sure if it's the game, or if it's that I'm spending the night at Jon's. His parents are out of town at some big convention in Vegas where his dad is speaking, so Jon invited us over after the game.

Because Tyler's been out all week Jon has been eating lunch with us more often—every day this week, in fact. Yesterday at lunch, I was talking about how great Jon was in the snippet of rehearsal I saw on Tuesday night. Monica said he's even better in the scene where they have their big duet.

"You've only heard him do 'Trouble,' which is really good," she said. "But his singing voice is amazing."

"I've heard him sing, too." I didn't really think about it before I said it.

"When?" Monica was looking at me, then over at Jon.

"When he was helping me study for my English test."

Jon started laughing. "Oh yeah. I forgot about that."

I told everybody how Jon had played the Boison song as a ballad, and the girls all made him promise to play it for them that night after the game when we were at Jon's place.

"I can also report that Jon is an excellent kisser," Monica said with a mischievous glint in her eye. "At least onstage. We'll have to ask Amy about other places."

Amy giggled and blushed. I glanced at Jon, who rolled his eyes and smirked at me while he shook his head.

"You kissing my girl onstage?" I asked.

"No tongue," he said. "It's barely a peck, but we hold our lips together for a while."

"It's a stage kiss, babe." Monica draped her arms around my neck. "Jealous?"

The weird thing is, I am jealous—but not of Jon, I don't think. I think I'm jealous of Monica. I wanna know what it's like to kiss Jon.

Shit. Did I just write that down?

All week long, I've just hung out with Jon and it's been so easy without Tyler here. Tracker and Watters and the rest of the guys think Jon is great, and they're all jazzed about the party at his place. With Tyler gone, I haven't been giving much thought to "what's going on with me." I've been reminding myself to just be me and go with my gut—exactly like I do on the field.

On the way into class, Erin said she was so excited because Tyler would be back next week. Thinking about that started my stomach on a slow boil. I realize now that I've written all this that I'm not nervous about the game—or even about Jon. I'm nervous about Tyler coming back to school.

All I can do is put that out of my head. It's not happening right now, so I shouldn't waste time worrying about it right now. At this moment, there's no problem. Jon is sitting across the aisle, Monica is sitting across the room, and I'm going to try for another passing record again tonight. Then there's a party at Jon's. That's what's going on right now.

So why don't I feel more in control? If everything is really okay, why doesn't it feel like it? Why do I feel like the floor is about to fall out from under me?

145

Saturday, September 22

I've been staring at this blank page forever. I don't even know how to start writing down what's happened in the past twenty-four hours. I feel like I'm splitting in two on the inside. There's this thinking part of me that needs to write this all down in order to make sense of it, and there's this feeling part of me that is running around like a crazy person—shouting and screaming and laughing and crying. The feeling part is afraid—afraid that if I write down what actually happened last night it will make it . . . real. It's like I'm staring at a movie of last night in my mind. Right now, if I keep it there in my head, nobody knows. But if I write it down, if I see it in my own handwriting on a page in this journal, it means that it exists—that it really happened, not just in my head.

And what really happened?

- We won the football game.
- I completed a lot of passes.
- I came close to breaking the passing record I set last week.
- The scouts were back, including two I'd never seen before.
- A camera crew showed up from Channel 7 to interview me and Coach afterward.
- We went to Jon's for a party.

But none of that is what *really* happened.

Sometimes the facts seem to boil down to one specific moment—the only thing that's happened all week, or all year, or maybe in my entire life that really matters. The other stuff has happened before. It happened last week. It'll happen again next week—some version of it, anyway.

But last night something *really* happened.

And I can't even write it down yet.

The thing is, I *need* to write it down. I know it. I need to write it down so that I can see it on the page and make sense of what happened somehow. Thinking about it only goes so far. I can watch it on the movie screen in my mind, but I can't really wrap my head around it. Writing it down will help me sort it out. It'll help me figure out what the play is—how to maneuver this pigskin of an experience into the end zone where it belongs. Writing it down will help me make it a win instead of a fumble.

But I can't do it.

Not yet.

Maybe if I write in the direction of what happened, I can get there. Maybe I can make a long, slow march down the field toward the end zone.

The kickoff was really when we all got to Jon's place. Sure, there was exciting stuff before: the game, the passing, the crowd, the thunderstorm at halftime, the cameras on the sideline draped with tarps and rain covers, sliding around in the mud on the field, the water flying off the ball as I flung it toward Tracker and Watters, the spray as one of them would catch it and dive into the giant mud puddle of an end zone, the fourth win in a row, the reporters excited about the undefeated season so far, and Alicia Stevenson, heels in one hand, umbrella in the other, walking me back to my car, promising me paperwork that very week, wondering when she could sit down with me to sign.

But the night really started at Jon's.

His house isn't far from mine and Monica's as it turns out—different end of the same neighborhood on the bluff overlooking the river. Only his house is higher up than either of ours. It's a big glass box with whole walls that are glass and slide open onto a deck that wraps all the way around the place. The roof is flat but seems to be propped up somehow, giving a steady rise toward a view of the Arkansas River and the endless sky.

The furniture inside is all really cool and retro. There are lighting fixtures that look like spaceships and low-slung sectionals that curve. The fireplace is stone and has a big metal sunburst piece of wall art on it. The big coffee table in the den curves like a boomerang.

The party was smaller than the rager at Monica's for my birthday. Maybe it was the rain, or maybe Jon didn't invite as many people, but by two a.m., it was just me and Jon and the bottle of Maker's Mark he'd pulled out of his dad's stash in the garage.

"Isn't your dad gonna miss this bottle?" I asked.

"Nah. He always gets bottles as gifts from the hospital. He doesn't drink much—only when we have company over, which isn't very often."

I can't imagine my dad drinking only when we had people over. In fact, I don't remember the last time my parents had friends of their own over. Usually it's just me and Tracy who have friends over. I wonder if Mom would have people over if Dad drank less. Maybe if he only drank when they had people over, Mom would have more people over.

Monica and Amy had not forgotten about Jon playing that Boison song, and they didn't shut up about it until he finally grabbed the guitar in the middle of the living room and performed for everybody.

Just like in my bedroom that night, Jon's voice was clear and strong, floating over the chords as he tapped his fingers to the rhythm beneath the strings. This time as he started singing he kept his eyes open and looked around the room. There was something about having an audience that was magical for Jon—his eyes were electric. His voice was flawless. The effect was mesmerizing. And then he got to the bridge and stared straight at me:

And
I don't know what happens now
But
I just have to tell you somehow

Those lines don't take very long to sing, and nobody seemed to notice, but I felt my pulse kick into high gear. It couldn't just be a coincidence that the two times I'd seen him sing this song, he stared right at me during those words, right?

As he got back to the chorus, he tossed his head back a little and closed his eyes:

You're the one I've always wanted
You're the one I've always wanted
You're the one I've always wanted
To love.

There was a hush over the room as Jon finished and then an explosion of mainly Monica squealing and the rest of the cheerleading squad rushing him. Amy got there first and had her arms around his neck, hugging him. The guys were all jealous as hell of the attention he was getting, but they couldn't deny he had skills.

"I guess I'll be going home to kill myself," Tracker said grimly, pouring us all another shot of Maker's.

"That white boy got skills." Sears shook his head. "Ladies love a man who can sing."

Sears and Tracker polished off, like, half the bottle between them, and Mike Watters told them he refused to drive them back to their cars at the school that night.

"We've got a good thing going," he said over their protests. "We're four and oh on the season, and we're not losing anybody to a DUI or worse." Monica had only had a single sip, and she and Amy left early because they had an all-day rehearsal for *The Music Man* today.

Finally, by two a.m., it was just me and him. We drank a little more. We laughed a lot. We polished off a pint of Ben & Jerry's apiece while watching TV. I told him I was fine to drive—that I really didn't need to stay the night.

He was rinsing out all the empty glasses in the kitchen sink when I said it. I saw a tiny frown crease his brow, but he shrugged it off. "Sure, man. Whatever works." He dried his hands, poured one more shot and knocked it back, then gazed at me across the island countertop and just waited.

I didn't know what to say, but I couldn't look away from those eyes. I felt the color rising in my cheeks. *Just be you. Just be you. What do* you *want to do?*

I *wanted* to stay, but it felt dangerous. It felt like if I stayed, something would be different between me and Jon—and not just me and Jon. It felt like everything would change.

"Don't you have to be up early tomorrow?" I asked him.

"Nah. Mr. London is blocking Monica's big solo tomorrow morning. My call time isn't until after lunch."

"You're really good onstage," I said.

He sort of laughed through his nose and put his glass in the sink, then ran a hand over his eyes and through his dark hair. A couple pieces fell back down across his forehead. He looked over at me again.

"I know," he said.

I laughed. "Wow. Modest, too."

He walked across the kitchen and hit the lights. The spots in the ceiling faded out, the whole room now bathed in the bluish glow of the LEDs under the stainless-steel range hood. This kitchen was like a movie set.

"I don't perform to be told I'm good," he said. "I do it because I love it." He walked into the living room.

"Where are you going?" I followed him.

He stopped at the foot of the short staircase that led to the hallway and the other side of the house. "To bed, man. Where are you going?"

His question hung in the air. I could make out the silhouette of his body standing by the stairs. The moonlight poured in through the wall of windows behind him. The curve of both shoulders spilled into his biceps. I couldn't see his face.

Could he see mine?

The air felt thick all of a sudden. I could hear my heart pounding in my ears. *Jesus. This is no big deal. He crashed at your place. Spend the night.*

"I guess I'll stay."

"Cool." Even in the dark, I could hear the smile in his voice. He turned and headed up the stairs. I followed, repeating to myself: *Just be you. Just be you.* As we walked into his room, I realized I had no idea who that was anymore.

Who am I?

Jon flipped on the light in the bathroom, then the floor lamp in the corner of his room. His bed was a king size, but his room was so big that there was plenty of space for a desk with a computer and a chair on wheels. At the other end of the room was a floor-to-ceiling window that had a view of the river. I could see the lights of the bridge over the dam where we'd hung out the week before. I turned around in time to see Jon pull his T-shirt off and toss it onto the ottoman that matched the cool black leather chair in the corner where I was standing. It looked like the place where the captain of a spaceship would sit.

"Nice view," I said. Jon stopped short and looked at me. It registered with me that he'd just taken off his shirt. I blushed. Hard. He laughed as he walked into the bathroom.

"Yeah, man. You can see the dam from here. Pretty cool, huh?" I heard the water running and Jon brushing his teeth. I

153

stood there, staring out the window. I could see the faint glow of my own reflection in the glass and then the lights along the river beyond. I took deep breaths and looked at my own eyes shining in the glass.

Who are you? Why does this feel so dangerous?

"Left a new toothbrush on the sink for you if you want it." Jon's voice startled me, and I almost jumped out of my skin. "Whoa! Sorry, man. Didn't mean to sneak up on you."

"It's cool." I tried to laugh it off.

Jon's smirk came unfurled like a flag across his face. "Usually, you're the one lurking out there in the dark."

"I didn't mean to lurk," I said. "I just heard the music— that's all."

Jon pulled open a drawer and tossed a piece of clothing my way. "Shorts if you want 'em." He unbuckled his belt and kicked off his sneakers at the same time. I practically ran into the bathroom, hearing his jeans come off behind me. All I could see was that image of his boxer briefs in my mind. I didn't want to get caught staring again, but part of me was disappointed I hadn't seen him take his jeans off.

I brushed my teeth, staring into my eyes in the mirror.

Just be you. Just be you. Just be you.

I rinsed and spat and hesitated.

Who am I?

I took a deep breath and ran a hand through my hair. It was sticking up every which way—sort of spiky the way I liked it. Monica says it looks like bed head. I pulled off my polo and stood in front of the mirror. I flexed my right arm and let my eyes wander over my biceps and down my abs. I had those lines that ran into the waistband of my jeans like those guys in the big black-and-white ads at the clothing stores in the mall. Monica would always giggle and wrinkle her nose when she touched my stomach.

Why did I care so much how I looked? I turned the water back and splashed some on my face; then I blotted it dry with a towel. I slid out of my jeans. I stood there and took one more quick glance at myself standing there in my boxers.

Should I put on these shorts? Is he wearing shorts?

I grabbed my clothes and the shorts Jon had given me and took a final deep breath, then opened the door and walked back into his room.

Jon was propped up in his bed, shirtless, on one elbow, tapping something into his phone. I tossed my clothes onto the chair, pulled back the sheet and comforter, and slid into the gigantic bed before I thought about it too much.

"Is it totally gay that we're sleeping in the same bed?" I asked.

Jon didn't answer right away. He put his phone on the nightstand and reached over to turn off the lamp by the bed.

I saw a flash of his lats as he did. *Swimming must be the best workout in the entire world.*

"Do you know any gay people?" My eyes were adjusting to the dark, but Jon's voice sounded like it was coming from far away. This bed was huge. There was no danger of us touching, but something about his question made the air thick in the room. I felt that familiar weight on my chest that I felt so often when I was alone with him. I rolled toward my side of the bed and hugged the pillow, punching it a couple of times.

"Actually, I do know one," I said. "Monica's uncle. Brent. He was at dinner at her place on Sunday."

"Huh." The lights from the bridge over the river floated in through the windows, turning Jon's room a dark blue. I saw him roll onto his back and put his hands under his head. "What was Brent like?" he asked.

I told him a little bit about Brent, but it was hard to breathe. I was lying in bed in my boxers talking to a dude about a gay guy I'd met. I was lying on my stomach, and I made sure to keep my left leg against the very edge of the mattress. I didn't want Jon to think I was trying to cuddle up.

"He actually seemed really . . . normal," I said. "He was funny, and way into baseball."

"Was he handsome?"

The minute Jon said this, my stomach did a somersault. All

of a sudden I was totally turned on. I couldn't move. I could barely speak. It felt like all the oxygen had been sucked out of the room. I squirmed against the sheets and finally choked out an answer. "I guess so. I mean, if you . . . Yeah, he's a good-looking guy."

Jon glanced over at me and smiled. The silence was killing me. I squeezed the pillow under my head to make my hands stop shaking. Why were my hands shaking? I had to keep talking. "He said he was having problems finding somebody to date. He had these hilarious stories about these guys he'd gone out with and how lame they were. He said the last one kissed like a weed eater."

Jon rolled onto his side, facing me, his arm bent underneath his head, his biceps and shoulder creating a pillow on top of his pillow. "Have you ever kissed a dude before?"

"No." My heart leaped into my throat. It felt like there was a power surge in the sheets, static flying through the air. I felt like I might explode. "Have you?" I croaked.

Jon just looked at me for a split second, and then somehow, he was right beside me, his hand on the side of my neck, his thumb resting on my jaw just like that one night at his Jeep when he was leaving. Only this time, he didn't turn away. He gently pulled my head toward his, and I felt his lips pressed against mine.

My whole body tensed, then relaxed into his. His mouth was firm and strong and warm against mine. The hum that seemed to flow through the sheets shot through my whole body, and Jon brought us closer together. I felt his leg and hip pressed against my leg and my hip. His tongue searched out mine for a moment, warm but not wet or sloppy. Sometimes when I kissed Monica, I felt like I was going to drown, but kissing Jon was so different. After a second he broke away, his hand still on my neck and jaw where it had been, his forehead against mine.

My eyes fluttered open. My breath was a ragged gasp. I wanted to lean forward, to kiss him again. For a moment we were frozen there—and then I realized what had just happened, and I felt my heart rate rocket like I'd just sprinted from one end zone to the other. I pulled away and jumped up out of the bed like I was being chased by a pack of rabid dogs.

"Jon!" I yelled his name. "I'm not gay."

Jon popped up and slowly swung his long legs over the edge of the bed, his hands out like I was holding him at gunpoint. "Hey, man. It's cool. It's cool." His voice was so calm. My heart was pounding. I could barely breathe. I glanced down at the front of my boxers and grabbed a pillow to hold it over myself. *Dammit.*

I backed up against the wall and slid down to the floor. Tears filled my eyes, and I buried my face in the pillow. "I'm not gay," I said over and over. Suddenly I was crying. "I can't be gay. I'm not gay."

Jon was silent, but even with my head buried in the pillow, I could sense him near me. After a minute I ran a hand over my face, brushing the tears away. I was so embarrassed, I could barely move.

When I dared to look up at Jon, he was staring straight at me, and the look on his face was so kind, and so warm, and so . . . him. When he caught my eyes, he spoke: "Nobody said you were gay."

I gave a short, bitter laugh. "Uh. We were just kissing in your bed. I think Tyler would say that's pretty fucking gay."

"Yeah, but Tyler isn't here, is he?" Jon's voice was steady and soothing. He smiled and rolled his eyes. "And who made Tyler the grand high poo-bah of everything? Who says he gets to decide what's gay and what isn't?"

I was quiet for a second. The bourbon and the crying made my head swim a little. I rubbed my eyes and looked back up at Jon. "It's just . . . I can't . . . I mean, if Tyler ever found out, I just . . ."

"Who's gonna tell him?"

Jon slid off of the bed and sat next to me on the floor. His white boxer briefs glowed blue in the light from the window. I felt his shoulder touch mine. After a minute he bumped my knee with his.

"Nobody's saying you're gay. Nobody's saying I'm gay. We're just two guys kissing."

I turned to face him. "It's not that simple. I—"

"Maybe not." He cut me off. "But it could be."

We sat there for what seemed like a long time, my head racing to match my heartbeat:

This is who you are. This is who you are. This is who you are.

All at once, I realized why I was really scared—not of people finding out, or What It All Means; I mean, I am plenty scared of that, too. But in that moment, I got terrified Jon might get up and never try to kiss me again. All I knew for sure was that I couldn't risk that.

But how did I tell him I wanted to kiss him again? How did I tell him I wanted to take him up on his offer to just be two guys messing around?

What were the right the words?

Before I could find them, Jon sighed and stood up. He looked so freaking tall standing over me like that. I let my eyes drink in what I hadn't dared to see before: how amazing he looked in his underwear. It was like he was a Greek god chiseled out of blue marble. I was afraid to move, afraid that if I said one more wrong word, he'd toss me my jeans and tell me to go home.

Instead Jon reached down and offered his hand. I took it, and he pulled me up. He didn't let go. Neither did I. That's how

I told him, with no words at all, our hands locked together between our chests, our noses so close I could feel his breath on my cheek.

"I don't wanna freak you out," he whispered. "I just wanna kiss you."

There was something so honest and so open in his eyes at that moment, I made a decision. It wasn't a decision to come out of the closet or be gay for the rest of my life, or anything like that. I just decided to trust him. I didn't even have to think about it—like being on the field and just knowing, seeing the whole spread in front of me and not taking a moment's hesitation before cocking my arm back for the pass. I knew exactly what my move was.

I pulled him toward me and kissed him again. I put both hands up to his face, and as I did, I felt his arms slowly wrap around my waist and draw me tightly against him. I'd never been held like that before.

Ever.

He pulled me down onto the bed, and our legs and arms and lips were all tangled up. We were breathing at the same time, the same air. There was a pulse between us in a way that I had never felt with Monica, or any of the other girls I'd kissed. Sure, I'd gotten turned on when I'd made out with girls. It's just that this was different from simply having a hard-on. That was just friction. This was like my brain and body and thoughts and heart all ran together with Jon's and I lost myself completely in this moment. It was like I'd been dying of thirst and finally felt myself falling headlong into a pool of the coolest, sweetest water I'd ever tasted.

At first I was scared to move my body at all. I kept my hands on his face and moving through his hair while he held me tightly against him. After a while he broke away from my lips and looked into my eyes, smiling.

"Damn. You're good at that."

I blushed. I didn't know what to say. He kissed me again, lightly on the lips. I was out of breath and panting a little. My whole body felt lit up like a carnival ride at night. I could barely look at him. We were pressed together so tightly. I knew he could feel what was going on in my boxers as clearly as I could feel what was going on in his. Finally I forced myself to bring my eyes to his eyes.

"Jesus," I whispered.

"What?" he asked.

"You're trouble."

He smirked. "Right here in River City."

All I could do was stare into his eyes as I let my hands wander down to his shoulders and across his biceps. I ran my fingers over his pecs and pulled away from him a little as my hand trickled down his abs to the waistband of his boxer briefs.

He grabbed my wrist. "Wait."

I looked back up at him and felt my cheeks go red. *Did I do something wrong?* "Sorry. I just—I mean, I was . . . ," I stammered.

He brought my hand up to his mouth and kissed it, then pressed his body into mine again.

"It's cool," he said. "I just think . . ." His voice trailed off. "Maybe we should take it slow?"

We made out for a while longer, until I felt my mouth getting a little raw from Jon's stubble.

I laughed. "My lips are getting chapped," I said.

He smiled. "Yeah. Mine too. Hazard of kissing guys, I guess." He rolled over and opened the drawer of his nightstand. He applied some lip balm, then handed it to me and jumped out of bed.

"Jesus, dude." He pulled at the front of his underwear. "You got me all riled up." He left the bedroom, and I heard him run down the stairs. A few seconds later he was back with a bottle of water. "I gotta get some shut-eye so I can sing tomorrow."

We took big gulps of the water, passing the bottle back and forth. Then I put it on the floor next to the bed. When I rolled back over, Jon was under the sheets, propped up on his elbow. He put his hand on my chest.

"You okay?"

An old panic returned when he said that. I reached up and grabbed his hand. "You can't tell anybody."

He pulled a pillow over toward my side of the bed, slid an arm under my pillow, and wrapped the other one around me. "Tell anybody what?"

"About . . . *this*," I said.

He yawned and settled in next to me, closing his eyes. "I don't even know what you're talking about."

"And I'm not your boyfriend."

"Uh . . . you have a girlfriend. And I have . . . Amy."

"I just—"

"Dude." He interrupted me and squeezed me really tightly to get my attention.

"Yeah?"

"Nobody's gonna hear about this from me. Got it?" He pecked me on the cheek. "Now shut up and go to sleep."

So.

That's what happened last night.

This morning, when I woke up, he was sitting on the edge of the bed, showered and dressed. The light was pouring in the window. It was after eleven a.m. His T-shirt said FLYING BURRITO BROTHERS, and when my eyes opened, he smirked and said he had to leave, but that I should just pull the front door closed behind me.

When he tried to stand up again, I grabbed his hand and pulled him back toward me. He came down on his knees next to the bed, laughing.

"Dang. You're strong."

I pulled his head close to mine and kissed him really long and hard. He leaned in to me, and I could taste his toothpaste and smell his deodorant, and I wanted to pull him back onto the bed. After we kissed for a minute, he put both hands on my shoulders and gently pushed me away.

He stood up over the bed and ran a hand through his hair with a big sigh. Then he fixed me with that amazing smirk and those incredible eyes and shook his head. "Trouble," he said.

Then he was gone.

I lay in his bed for a long time, thinking about what happened last night and just then. Finally I got up, got dressed, and drove home.

Dad was on the couch watching the U of A game when I walked through the door. I sat there staring at the screen with him for a long time. We've always hunted and watched football together. Something about sitting there next to him felt right, but now it also felt horribly wrong, too. There was something unseen between us—this huge thing that I don't even understand.

I mean, I understand it intellectually. Hell, I've been flipping through books about "changes to your body" since I was in sixth grade, looking up the chapters on what it means to experience "same-sex attraction." Even before I knew, I guess I *knew*.

But now I *know*. I *really* know. I know from *experience*.

And there's no way I can go back to *not* knowing. I'll always know this about myself, and I'll never be able to tell my dad. How will I always be able to hide this from him?

I sat there on the couch until halftime, and then I came up here to my room to write this all down. All I can think about is how my dad can *never* know and at the same time, about how much I want to kiss Jon again.

My lips are still chapped, and every time I touch them, I feel excited and scared. I want to laugh and cry at the same time.

I have to go for a run.

Sunday, September 23

In church.

Bored as hell.

Tried to send Jon twenty different texts yesterday, but none of them sounded right, so I deleted them all. I thought maybe he'd text me after rehearsal, but he didn't. I went for my run, and as I got out of the shower, Monica pulled up with Amy and said we were meeting Jon for food. I guess I got really excited, because Monica said, "There it is."

"There *what* is?" I asked her.

"Your smile," she said. Then she leaned in to kiss me, and I sort of pulled my head back as if I were saying, *What are you doing?* But then I caught what I had done right as she gave me this funny look. I turned my head quickly to the side and coughed. I played the whole thing off as though I had been about to cough in her face. Then I leaned in and kissed her.

I tried to really kiss her the way I had kissed her before— the way I had kissed Jon yesterday morning before he left for rehearsal. It felt like putting on sunscreen after you're already fried: too little, too late.

But I think it just felt that way to me. Monica seemed to really be into it. Amy was not.

"Jeez, you guys. Get a room."

Amy isn't really known for her originality, but I was glad to have an excuse to get into the car.

Jon was waiting for us on the deck outside at the restaurant, and he smiled as I slid into the chair next to his, but during dinner he barely talked to me. He mainly talked to Monica about the musical and Amy about meeting her family down at the River Market for lunch today. When I finally got up the nerve, I scooted my leg over under the table so my knee touched his, but just then he got up and said he had to use the restroom.

When he came back, the girls decided to go to the restroom together, and I had the chance to ask him if he was okay.

"Totally," he said.

"Cool. I guess—I thought maybe you'd call or something after rehearsal."

He just said, "Slowly," but he winked and smiled at me when he said it. Then he squeezed my knee under the table.

At that very moment the waiter showed up with our food (of course), and then the girls came back. I tried for the rest of the meal to figure out a way to arrange it so that Jon would take me home and Monica would take Amy home, but there was really no way to make that happen without it being weird. Jon took Amy home and gave me a fist bump as I got into Monica's car.

"Catch ya Monday" was all he said. I felt my stomach turn. *Monday?*

"You okay?" Monica asked before she started the car. I didn't know how to answer. So I just leaned across the seat and kissed her until she giggled and pushed me off.

I kissed her some more when we got back to my place, but when I tried to slide my hand up her shirt, she batted me away and told me that she had to get home.

"To do what?" I asked, secretly relieved.

I honestly don't remember what she said now. All I could think about was texting Jon. I was doing that as I passed my dad in the hallway.

"Always glued to that damn phone, boy. Gotta get you out in the woods. Get you away from all that pansy-ass technology. Give you a good ol'-fashioned rifle."

Pansy ass?

Every time I pass my dad in the hall now, I get scared that he can tell. It's stupid, I know. Like what? He's the giant from Jack and the Beanstalk? He can somehow *smell* the gay on me?

Jon didn't text me back last night. And nothing this morning.

Jesus. I'm losing my fucking mind.

In church.

Monday, September 24
English—First Period

Tyler is back. He had surgery last Monday, and he's already been to physical therapy twice. He says they're being really aggressive with it so that he can get back in shape by spring. He's still on crutches and wearing a big brace, but he actually smiled at me this morning and said he was going to come to practice and watch this afternoon for a little bit before he has to go to physical therapy.

Jon came in late this morning, so I didn't get a chance to talk to him yet. I texted him yesterday to see how things went with Amy on Saturday night, but he just texted:

It was fine. =P

Then . . . nothing.

I am trying not to let it bother me. I am trying not to text him every ten minutes. I mean, I'm the one who made it clear that I didn't want him to get all clingy and start thinking of me as his boyfriend or something.

What is happening?

What if I'm the clingy one?

Tuesday, September 25

Jesus. What a couple of days.

So, yesterday afternoon, when Tyler came to practice to hang out for a few minutes before physical therapy, we were running tackles and doing burpees when I saw these guys sitting near him in the bleachers. I just assumed they were the PT team his dad has him set up with trying to get him back in shape.

Then, after a while, I glanced over and Tyler was gone but these guys were still there. They were watching us run line drills and had stop watches out. One of them was talking to Coach on the sideline.

After I got out of the shower and was headed out of the locker room, I passed Coach's office and he stuck his head out the door after me.

"You going to talk to 'em?"

"Who?" I asked.

"Those scouts."

"What scouts?" I asked.

Coach smiled for what might be the second time in his entire life—at least that I've ever seen. "You'll see," he said. "Talk to 'em."

When I walked out the door, I saw both of the guys who were in the bleachers. Both of them were really tan, and the tall, blond one stepped forward and introduced himself. They were scouts.

"Dave Joseph, USC."

I shook his hand. "Hey." These guys were from California?

"You got a second?"

I nodded. "You came here from California; guess I have a second."

"We were in Memphis visiting a couple guys."

"And you just happened over to Little Rock?" I asked.

"We were here in May," he said. "Spring eval looking at Tyler."

I remembered seeing Tyler talking to the guys in the bleachers at the start of practice. "Did you make him an offer?" I asked.

"He was pretty dead set on sticking around here," Dave said. "Besides, I read about his injury online. Then I saw some footage of you. You haven't given anybody a verbal yet, have you?"

I shook my head. "OU offered, but when she came back last week, I sort of didn't get a chance to talk to her."

Dave frowned. "Alicia Stevenson? She's been to see you twice?"

"Three times. I talked to their coach last spring. I just figured . . ."

Dave held up his hand. "Don't tell me anything else. I don't wanna know. This is technically 'Quiet Period.' She's supposed to see you only once in person until November."

I nodded. I'd heard about this, but I didn't think it counted unless it was the coach of the team.

"Don't be fooled by the long legs and the high heels, man. OU is great and all, but we're talking PAC-12. State school versus private."

"Are we talking that?" I asked.

He smiled. "This is my one chance face-to-face. You see me?" He waited until I looked him in the eye. "We want you. We need a QB with a passing game. You're our guy. You do what you want, but have you been to Oklahoma City?"

I nodded. "Once. As a kid. Drove through on the way to my mom's cousin's wedding."

He laughed. "It hasn't gotten any better, trust me. Los Angeles is where you want to be."

He held out his hand again. I shook it. There was a business card pressed into my palm.

"Don't get stuck in the Midwest, man. Come to LA. We'll make you a star. It's what we do there."

As I watched them stride away across the field toward the parking lot, I felt my phone buzz in my bag. When I pulled it out, I had a text from Tyler:

```
USC, huh? Nice!
```

I called him and could hear the genuine excitement in his voice. I knew it was mainly because he knew I wouldn't take his Arkansas deal any longer. And he was right. I laughed with Tyler for the first time in a long time. I asked him how his knee was, and he said it hurt like a bitch, but that he was in it to win it.

Alicia Stevenson must've gotten tipped off. She called my cell three times today and left voice mails at home, too. When I got home from school today, Dad was all over it.

"You don't wanna move to the Left Coast with all those fairies, do you?"

Literally, that's what he said. Not "good work" or "amazing job" or "it's incredible that you've got three schools fighting over you now." It all came down to California and fairies.

I knew the minute I heard they were from USC that this was my chance—not just to play college ball, but my chance to get out of here. Out of the South in general. I don't need my dad's permission to take a scholarship. I'm eighteen years old. This is where I start to decide what I want for my own life. This is my decision, not his.

This is how it happens.

I texted Jon about it. He's calling me right now.

Later . . .

Just got off the phone with Jon. He may be more amped up about the USC offer than I am. It made me feel so good to get really excited about it with him. Suddenly I wasn't worried about what had been going on between us. I was just happy to be sharing good news with my friend. And he had news for me, too.

"You know, I've been looking at UCLA."

"Get the hell out!" I was almost shouting.

"True story," he said.

"For swimming?" I asked.

"Are you kidding? You're the world-class athlete. They've got a decent English program and a decent music program. I'm not really sure what I want to major in, but I know I want do it in LA."

In a flash I saw the whole thing: We could escape to LA together. I felt silly right away. *Are you planning happily ever after? He'll hardly look at you since last weekend.*

I took a deep breath. "Dude, since I . . . crashed at your

174

place the other night, has everything been . . . okay?"

He hemmed and hawed for a little while: homework, writing assignments, rehearsals . . .

Finally I said, "Spill it. What's going on?"

"I've just been . . . busy."

"Okay." The way I said it, he knew I wasn't buying whatever it was he was selling.

He sighed. "Look, I just . . . I didn't want you to feel like I was pressuring you."

This made me smile. Somewhere deep inside of me, it made me like Jon even more. "Pressuring me?" I said. "You're hardly talking to me."

"I just don't want you to think I'm making this something that it isn't." He said this slowly, like he was trying to choose exactly the right words.

"What *is* this?" I blurted out.

"I don't know." His voice was soft—like he wasn't sure what to say next.

"I don't know either," I said. "But I don't want it to stop."

I waited for him to say something for what seemed like an eternity. The air across the line was like a freight train.

Finally I heard him take a deep breath. "Me neither," he said.

"So . . . maybe you should talk to me in the halls or something?" I suggested. Jon laughed, and I felt relief splash over me like jumping into the pool on a hot day. "Whatever else you are, you're my friend first," I said. "Don't forget that part."

"Deal," he said. "See you tomorrow?"

"If you're lucky."

"You're trouble," he said.

"With a capital T."

Wednesday, September 26
English—First Period

Jon stopped by my locker this morning on the way to class. Monica and Amy were with him as usual, but it was different this morning. He actually looked me in the eyes and talked to me.

The Music Man opens this weekend, so Monica and Jon will be missing the game on Friday night. Then a bunch of us are supposed to go see it together on Saturday night. Mom has even got Dad to agree to come. She told him all about how Monica is the lead, but then she talked about what an amazing voice Jon has. I think it's a pretty safe bet that she and Tracy are more excited about seeing Jon sing than they are about seeing Monica.

I probably shouldn't admit this, but that's makes three of us.

I'm calling USC to give them a verbal agreement today. I haven't really told anybody yet. I'm just going to do it. For the first time in my life, I have the power to actually make something happen for myself. I have the power to decide who

I will be, where I will go . . . and when I think that Jon will be there, too, in a dorm across town . . .

I have this daydream that after our freshman years we get an apartment together somewhere off campus. What would it be like to wake up and see him standing there in his boxer briefs every morning? What would it feel like to crawl into bed next to him every night?

Jesus. I've spent only one night in an actual bed next to him and I'm already grinning like a moron while I write about it. That's way too much. It's way too far down the line. I can't even let myself think about that.

Head in the game.

Call USC.

Give a verbal agreement to play for them. I'll sign my letter of intent in February. National signing day is February 6 this year. Then it won't matter what my dad says. Or what anybody says. I'll be headed to California next fall.

With Jon.

Friday, September 28
English—First Period

Tough team tonight. North Hall is still undefeated too. One of us is going down. I'm less nervous about that than I am about tomorrow night. Going to see the musical with my parents has turned into an avalanche of worlds colliding.

That sounds way more dramatic than it is, probably.

Monica announced yesterday at lunch that her mom and Brent would be coming to the show tomorrow night. She wants us all to go out for dessert afterward. Tyler and Erin are going to come too, which makes me nervous. I just don't think Tyler has ever really hung out with an out gay guy before, and I don't want him to say anything stupid in front of Brent. Plus, I'm not sure how my parents are going to deal with him. It's just . . . a lot.

Why do I want to control this?

Why do I think I should? Or that it's even possible?

I can't control what these people do or say any more than I can control whether we win or lose out there tonight. I can only control what I do on the field—not what anybody else does. I can throw a hundred perfect passes, but if Tracker or Watters don't catch them, or if Sears doesn't block well and I get sacked, there's nothing I can do about that.

If Tyler freaks out or my dad gets drunk and acts like a moron, what can I do about that? Nothing. So why do I always pressure myself to manage all these people? It's like I think it's my job to run the freaking universe. Not only is it not my job, but I can't do it. When I try, I just end up disappointing myself and getting pissed off at all the people around me.

I don't want to be disappointed. That's what it comes down to. I don't want to lose. I don't want people to not like me. Somehow, if my dad or Tyler bags on Brent tomorrow night, it's not Brent that I'm worried about. It's me.

I want to talk to Jon about this, but we barely see each other. I hung around and waited for him last night after practice. They are all in dress rehearsals this week, and so they only got a half-hour break for dinner.

I drove him and Monica and Amy down to Sonic. He got the double bacon cheeseburger with fries and a gigantic cherry limeade. The girls both got grilled chicken wraps and diet Cokes. Monica was sitting up front, so I barely got to see him, but just knowing that Jon was behind me in the truck felt like it turned the temperature up in my whole body.

I handed Jon's food over the seat to him, and when he took it, he grabbed my hand and held it for a second. Nobody saw this—it happened so fast—but it made my night.

Monica laughed as I drove them back to campus.

"What are you so smiley about?" she asked.

"Nothing. Just fun to hang out with you guys." It wasn't really a lie. "I barely get to see you anymore 'cause you've always got play practice."

All three of them said it at once: "REHEARSAL!"

Jon texted me after I dropped them off:

Don't forget to get Monica flowers for
opening night.

I texted back:

Is that a thing?

Jon:

Yes. #yourehopeless

Me:

wanna kiss you again

Jon:

backatcha. Flowers. Don't forget.

Later . . .

I told Mom I wanted to get Monica some flowers for opening
night. She thought that was really sweet and got all crazy and
gushy about it. She ordered them from a florist to have them
delivered. I told her I was just going to swing by the grocery

180

store and get some roses or something and drop them off in the dressing room, but Mom wouldn't hear of it. So, Monica is getting a dozen roses tonight.

Later I decided to get Jon some flowers at the grocery store after school. They had lots of different kinds, but I wasn't sure what to get. I just knew I didn't want to give him roses. That just seemed not like *him*. It felt sort of mushy and weird. I guess the idea of giving another boy flowers is mushy and weird, and I almost left without getting any. Then I saw these bright yellow tulips, and I thought they looked less frilly and more bright and encouraging. They seemed like flowers you might give a friend instead of somebody you were in love with.

Jesus. That's a stretch. I mean, what is up with me? I'm a dude buying tulips for another dude.

But I did. I just didn't want him to think I didn't care about this.

Of course, when I got them back to school, I realized I couldn't actually write a note on them. I mean, what if somebody found it and read it and recognized my handwriting? Even if I didn't put my name on it, it was too risky. Plus, as I got out of my truck, I looked toward the doors of the theater and there was somebody or a group of people hanging out at every single entrance.

Then I saw Erin. She was talking to a couple of the other

girls in our class who are in the musical by the backstage door. So I called her over and gave them to her.

"Ooooh! Are these for Monica?" she asked. She said it like this was just the sweetest thing ever.

"No, I had Monica's delivered. They should already be here."

"Oh," she said. "Who did you get these for?"

I stood there staring at her like a jackass. *Think. Think. Think.* "I didn't get these, actually. They're for Jon."

She smiled slyly. "Oh! That Amy!" she squealed. "She's a *tricky* one." She grabbed the flowers and whispered, "I'll sneak them in and put them on his dressing table backstage."

"Thanks," I said. I smiled and winked at her like we were pulling off a bank heist. "Not a word to anybody," I said. "Don't even tell Amy you know about it."

Erin pantomimed locking her lips with a tiny key and tossing the key over her shoulder. Then she turned and half skipped over to the back of the theater and disappeared inside.

I smiled as I watched her go, then headed for the locker room to suit up.

We won. It wasn't easy, but we did it. North Central has a tough defensive line and they came prepped to shut down our passing game. Tracker and Watters were double-teamed most of the time, and it forced me to scramble and run a lot. I'm feeling pretty banged up from winding up on the bottom of the pile a lot more than usual.

We were tied at fourteen each when Sears wrestled a fumble away from their quarterback and we had a final chance with three minutes left at our own thirty-yard line. I knew I had to get Casey inside their thirty if I wanted a sure bet.

So I did it.

Maybe it was the momentum of the fumble going our way, or maybe it was just Tracker turning on the power and getting open, but I nailed two twenty-yard passes in a row right at him, and he caught them both. Boom: thirty-yard line. By that point, their defense had wised up and shut Tracker down again. I threw one pass out of bounds to stop the clock and then gained another four yards running before Casey sauntered out on the field and kicked an easy field goal with twenty-four seconds left in the game.

Afterward Coach came to find me in the locker room while I was pulling off my pads.

"So," he said, eyebrows raised. "Two more camera crews out there tonight, and Arkansas guys are here watching North Central's running back. Funny thing, though . . . Surprising absence of scouts hanging out by our locker room doors tonight."

I kept stashing my gear. I didn't want to tell him about USC yet.

"You stonewalling me here?" He laughed. "Okay. Fine. But don't think I don't know when my best player has made a verbal. Not my first time at this rodeo."

I looked up at him with a shrug and a smile. "Maybe they're just tired of watching us smoke the competition."

"USC?" he asked. It hadn't occurred to me before that he might be excited about one of his players heading to a college in a different conference. I looked him in the eyes and saw something I hadn't seen there before: hope.

I did my best version of Jon's smirk. "Maybe."

He leaned in closer. "Your parents on board?" Coach knew my dad from church and hunting. Dad's crew had even closed in a porch on Coach's house when I was in junior high.

"Maybe."

He shook his head with a smile. "You got balls, son." He turned to go but stepped back toward me. "None of my business, I know, but if your old man gives you any hassle about going away to school . . . you let me know?"

He didn't wait for a response, just whacked my butt with his clipboard as he left.

I took my time in the shower. I didn't feel like talking to anybody. Jon was the only one I really wanted to see, and I knew he and Monica were doing the show tonight. As I headed to my truck, the parking lot was still packed over by the theater, and I dumped my bag in my SUV, then headed over and walked into the lobby. I could hear music coming through the doors at the back of the theater, so I snuck up and opened one very slowly, slipping into the walkway behind the last row of seats under the balcony.

Jon was onstage with Monica, holding both of her hands in his, singing a song about how there had been birds and flowers and music all around him everywhere, but he'd never noticed them until he'd met her. Then, just as he was about to lean in for a kiss, they were interrupted by a bunch of kids playing band instruments—really badly. It was sort of hilarious, and amazing, and I actually forgot about how tired I was and how much my arms and legs ached from being pummeled on the field tonight. I just stood there in the back with this big smile on my face, laughing along with the rest of the audience.

At the end, the lights came up on the stage and everybody took a bow. Jon and Monica bowed last, and everybody in the audience stood up for them and clapped and cheered. I don't know why, but my eyes filled up with tears when that happened. I ducked back out the door and got into the parking lot before anybody saw me.

I saw Jon's Jeep when I was pulling out of the lot. I parked next to it and decided to wait for him to come out. It took so long that I actually nodded off with my engine running, listening to the radio. When he knocked on the window, I jumped.

"Sorry," he said when I rolled down my window.

"No worries." I smiled.

Jon reached out and slid his hand under my elbow where it was propped on the window. I wondered if maybe he'd been thinking about touching me as much as I was thinking about touching him. Just feeling his fingers under my forearm made my breathing shallow.

He smirked. He knew exactly what he was doing. "How was the game?"

"Rough, but we won. Show go well?"

He smiled. "It was awesome."

"Seemed like it. You got a standing ovation."

He frowned. "How did you . . . ?" He stopped. "No. You didn't."

"What?"

"You came in after the game and watched the end of the show?" He pulled his hands back and threw them both into the air, shaking his firsts into the sky. It was the funniest thing I'd ever seen him do.

"I couldn't help it!"

"Now you know the ending!" he yelped. "That is *not* the way this is supposed to go."

"I'm sorry! I'll forget the ending. Just for you!"

He slid both hands under my arm and pulled himself forward on the door. His face came dangerously close to mine. "You better," he whispered.

"Whatcha doing now?" I asked.

"Opening night cast party," he said. "Mr. London is throwing it at his place. I'd invite you, but it's sort of a cast-only thing."

My heart sank. "Do you have to go?" I asked.

Jon laughed. "Uh, yeah. I'm playing the Music Man in a musical called *The Music Man*. So, yes. I do have to attend the cast party."

Jon leaned back and stuck his head out from between the back of his Jeep and my SUV, taking a quick peek both ways. "Tomorrow night? I'm all yours." Then he leaned in the window and kissed me.

"Dude . . ." I wanted to yell at him, but I couldn't. I was weak in the knees. "You're gonna get us in trouble," I whispered.

"Nah." He winked. "See you tomorrow night."

I'm still so horny from that kiss, I can't sleep. Only one thing to do about that . . .

Saturday, September 29

Tonight was one of those nights where everything starts out normal and then at a certain point it just leaves the reservation. Suddenly you're hanging on for dear life, trying to get your horse to slow the hell down, but secretly loving the ride.

That probably makes zero sense. Let me see if I can even get it all down on the page.

Okay, first off, *The Music Man* was pretty great. I mean, not everybody was good in it, but luckily, Jon and Monica were awesome, and the band was solid too. Jon is incredible onstage. His voice is so big—even when he was singing softly, he completely filled the theater. Monica has a great voice too. When they sang "Till There Was You," I looked over and my mom was actually crying.

So was I.

I hadn't forgotten the ending of the show before I saw it again, but it was good to see it in context. Jon played a conman with a heart of gold who falls in love with the town librarian, played by Monica. Monica's character (Marian) protects Jon's character (Harold) from being found out by the authorities. He's swindling all the parents in town to pay for instruments for their kids, and then he's going to run out on them without teaching their kids how to actually play the instruments like he promised.

Something about meeting Marian and falling in love with her changes everything about him.

I've never seen a full musical live and in person before, let alone one that Jon was performing in. He has the instincts and skill of the very best quarterback who has ever played—only instead of running, jumping tackles, and throwing the ball, he's singing, cracking jokes, and dancing. It was amazing to watch. I sort of forgot that it was *him*. He was like this different character—which I guess is the whole point of acting.

Then, when he kissed Monica and sang "Till There Was You," all I could think about were those two times he looked right at me while he was singing that Boison song. I couldn't help thinking that maybe he was singing *these* words from *this* song to me as well—even though he was looking at Monica.

It crashed over me like a wave—how much I liked Jon and how differently everything looked in my life since he'd shown up in English class that first week with wet hair and handed me a pen. Maybe there really had been love all around me, but I'd never noticed it "till there was Jon."

Hahahaha! God, so cheesy, I know! I should just burn this journal right now.

I mean, what is *wrong with me?* Whatever. I can't help it. I sat there tonight with tears in my eyes listening to Jon sing. I was scared shitless that my dad would turn and look at me and see that I was about to cry. But he didn't. In fact, he was nodding off. Dad wasn't so thrilled about going to see a musical in the first place. He and Mom had taken me and Tracy out for Italian food before the show. He'd had at least three glasses of wine, and Mom had wound up driving the car to the theater.

Afterward, when the final song died away and the curtain came down, the whole crowd jumped up and clapped and cheered. When Jon came out for his bow, he was smiling and he waved up at the balcony, then looked right at where I was sitting and bowed. I don't know if he could actually see me or not, but it looked like he winked right at me when he bowed.

Afterward we went for dessert at this milk shake place that's open late. It's sort of like a fifties diner, with these huge booths and a soda fountain. We all slid around one that had seating on three sides of the table. Somehow Jon and I managed to land next to each other in the booth, with Monica on one side and Amy on the other. Tyler and Erin were there, along with my mom and dad, Monica's uncle Brent, and her mom, Barbara.

Once we were all sitting down, we ordered enough ice cream and milk shakes to sink a ship. Then Monica made introductions.

"Good to see you again." Brent smiled at me. "Been checking on the games since I was here. Nice passing record."

"Just gotta get him signed to Oklahoma," Dad jumped in.

"Where the wind comes sweeping down the plain," Brent quoted.

"'Scuse me?" said Dad, confused.

Jon smiled. "It's a lyric. From the musical *Oklahoma*."

"That's the show Brent did his senior year in high school," Barbara said.

"When God was a young boy," Brent joked. "Enough about ancient history."

The waiter appeared with our milk shakes in all sorts of crazy flavors. Brent raised his glass and proposed a toast: "To Monica and Jon! The stars of the show!" There were general hoots and shouts and whistles. Then everybody started talking at once.

Brent leaned over to Jon. "You killed it up there, man."

"Thanks," said Jon.

"Acting isn't easy. You have to really know who you're singing to in order to make musical theater work like that."

"I meant every word." As Jon said this, I felt his hand slide over my knee under the table. I could feel my cheeks get warm, but I just smiled and put an arm around Monica.

"And *you*," I said to her. "You were amazing."

"No, *you* are amazing," she said. "Those flowers you got me were gorgeous! They were the nicest flowers anybody got in the whole cast!"

"I dunno," said Jon. "I got some pretty cool flowers too." He smiled at Amy when he said this, but of course, she had no idea what he was talking about.

"That's so nice!" she said. "Who got them for you?"

I looked at Erin and gave her big wide eyes. *Don't. Say. A. Word.*

She smiled and blushed, but she didn't blow my cover. Note to self: Never play cards on a team with Erin. Zero poker face.

Jon smirked at Amy, thinking she was playing coy, and shrugged. "Oh, I don't know. Perhaps I have a secret admirer."

"You both deserve all the flowers you can carry," Mom said from over her chocolate malt. "I mean, my goodness, Boyd, didn't you just think Monica and Jon had the best chemistry onstage?"

Dad barely grunted as he slurped down his strawberry milk shake. Musicals were not his thing. This was clear.

"Well, thank God Jon showed up this year," said Monica. "Otherwise, I'd have gotten stuck with Bobby Crenshaw. That would've been a nightmare."

The minute she said his name, Tyler snorted with laughter. "That little faggot couldn't act like he was into you if you paid him a million dollars."

When he said the word "faggot," it was like someone had dropped a hydrogen bomb in the middle of the table. Barbara gave him a frosty glare, and I saw Brent's eyes narrow, but just for a second. Jon slowly pulled his hand off my knee under the table, as I felt Monica almost come out of the booth across the table.

"God, Tyler. You're such an idiot," she said. Loudly. Very loudly. I put a hand on her shoulder.

"Why?" he challenged her. "Because I'm the only one here

192

who doesn't think musicals are the highest form of entertainment in the world?" He turned to look at Brent. "How many musicals did you do in college, anyway?" he asked with a sneer.

Brent smiled at him and crunched a piece of ice from his glass of Coke before he answered. "All the musicals were in high school, actually," he said. "Didn't have time to do any more after I got to Ole Miss. Full-ride football scholarship takes up a lotta time."

Tyler frowned. "You played football for Ole Miss?"

"All-American running back, all four years." Brent wasn't flustered by Tyler at all. I was about to crawl out of my skin.

"No fooling!" said Dad. "I remember seeing you on TV. Brent . . . Nichols?"

Brent smiled. "That's me."

"Well, Barbara, you didn't tell me you had football royalty in the family." Mom smiled and winked. "Now, tell me, Brent. Are you married?"

"Actually, no. Just broke up with my boyfriend."

If the bomb had been dropped earlier, this was the explosion that set the room on fire. I pictured a mushroom cloud over our table as my dad stared into his empty glass like it was his job. Tyler snorted again.

My mother had not expected this, but there's something about Southern women: They are never at a loss for words, especially not when it comes to being gracious in an awkward social situation.

193

She shot Tyler a look that could've wiped out a continent and then turned to Brent with her best church smile. "I'm so sorry to hear that. Now, what is it that you do for work, Brent?"

"Pharmaceutical sales," Monica piped up.

"But I really miss being in musicals," said Brent with a breezy nonchalance. He seemed to be perfectly at ease with this conversation even though the rest of us were dying. "Monica, maybe next summer when you're home from college we should find a summer stock company and audition."

"Do you miss playing football?" Tyler sneered.

This time Brent laughed. I was shocked. He actually looked like he was enjoying himself. He looked at Tyler and raised his eyebrows. "Do you?"

Tyler turned red in the face. "Oh, I'll be playing again. My physical therapist says I'll be off these crutches end of next week, God willing."

Brent's smile stayed in place, but there was a cold snap in his eyes. "And is God . . . *willing*?" he asked Tyler.

"He sure is happier about me playing football than he is about you playing around with dudes."

Brent laughed hard at this comment. "Dunno about that, Tyler. I'm in the College Football Hall of Fame for rushing, and you're . . . well . . . you're in physical therapy. If we're looking at what makes God happy, you might want to rethink some things."

Brent stood up and leaned down to give Monica a kiss on the cheek. "You were a superstar tonight, sweetheart." He reached across me and stretched out a hand to Jon, who smiled up at him and shook it. "And you, sir, rendered me speechless. Best night at the theater in a long time." He squeezed Barbara's shoulder. "I've already covered the check with the waiter, Sis, so my treat."

Brent started to leave, but he turned around and smiled right at me. "Congrats on the season, man. USC is lucky to have you."

My stomach dropped as my dad's head popped up. "USC?" He looked at me. "What is he talking about?"

I shrugged and stammered. "I . . . I don't know. . . . I mean, they offered, and . . ."

"And you committed on Wednesday." Brent held up his phone. "They tweeted it earlier. Way to go, man. Get outta here while you can. Cali is a step in the right direction."

Then he was gone.

There was silence around our table as everybody stared at me. Just as my dad started to open his mouth, I felt Jon slide his hand back onto my knee. I held up my hand to stop him. "Dad. It's done. I'm committed."

It was the first time I'd ever actually stood up to him, and I was sitting down in a booth with Monica on one side, her arm wrapped through mine, and Jon on the other, his hand firm on my leg. I never realized how much strength I take from my friends. Without them, I don't know how I would've survived that moment. I don't think I'd have had the courage to stop the tongue-lashing before it began.

After a moment, Mom dove in again. Gotta love a good hostess. Never let the conversation die. "Well, boys. It's about that time of year," she chirped. "Tyler, are you getting excited about the big hunting trip next month?"

Tyler shook his head and glanced up at her. "No, ma'am," he said. "Won't be able to make it this year."

"Well, surely you'll be off your crutches by then," Mom said.

"Yes, ma'am, but I'll be in physical therapy hard-core for the next few months. If I want a shot at getting my scholarship offer reinstated, I have to be in the best shape of my life in the spring."

"We don't have to do the trip this year." My dad sounded like a man who was lost in his own country.

"Nonsense," my mom clucked. "Jon, you'll have to go this year. You can take my bow if you want to."

I tried not to look at Tyler's face, but I saw him roll his eyes.

Jon glanced at my dad. "Well, if you guys want me along, I'm happy to join you."

"Sure thing," I said. "It'll be fun."

Dad looked at me blankly. I smiled to encourage him. He

nodded. "Sounds great," he said. "I'll see if Randall and the guys from the crew want to come along too."

Monica wrinkled her nose and pecked me on the cheek. "You're on your own, smelly boys. Sleep in tents. Kill beautiful animals. Amy and I will be camping out in my living room that weekend."

Barbara smiled. "Lifetime movies and pedicures for all. Erin, you're welcome to join us whether Tyler goes off into the woods or not."

The girls talked about planning that weekend until we headed home. I don't remember anything else that was said. All I could hear were the words "Cali is a step in the right direction." All I could feel was the heat of Jon's hand on my leg.

When we left the restaurant, Jon offered to take Monica and Amy home, and I jumped in with them. We dropped the girls off first, then drove toward my place. Instead of heading up the hill, toward the neighborhood, Jon steered us down to the park by the bridge over the dam. Technically, the parking lots are closed at dark, but he pulled off on a wide shoulder down past the bridge and turned off his lights.

He had the top off his Jeep, and in the quiet you could hear the water rushing by. We sat there really quietly for a little while, just watching the lights and listening to the water.

"Thanks for the flowers."

I looked at him and smiled in the dark. The light from the bridge and the moon shone back at me in his eyes. "How'd you know?" I asked. I could barely talk. Something about sitting there had me totally turned on.

"Oh, c'mon. Who else was gonna give me flowers and not leave a note? Then Amy asked who gave them to me, and Erin almost had an aneurism across the table tonight."

"I just . . ." I was blushing, and I didn't know what to say. Did he think they were lame? That it was too girly or something? I thought about standing up to my dad. Talking to Jon was way easier. I just had to find my voice. "I just wanted you to know that I was thinking about you."

Jon didn't say another word. He unbuckled his seat belt, opened his door, and grabbed the roll bar, swinging all six feet, three inches of himself over the side of the Jeep and into the backseat. I looked back, and he patted the seat next to him.

"C'mere."

I followed.

We kissed for a long time. Jon pulled me down on top of him, and we were pressed tightly against each other, the force of our legs and arms pulling tighter, our hips grinding into each other, until I couldn't tell where he stopped and I started. We got lost in each other.

It's funny, I don't remember getting lost when I was making

out with Monica. I was always wondering if I was doing it right, or thinking about how wet my face was getting, or worried about squishing her if I rolled over the wrong way.

I don't think about any of that when I'm making out with Jon. I don't think about anything. It's all I can do to remember to keep breathing, and sometimes I forget to do even that. Every once in a while one of us would pull back, sort of gasping for breath. One time when this happened, Jon pushed me back, and we both sat up. I hopped up and sat on the back of the backseat, pulling off my shirt. It was sweaty, and I was having a hard time catching my breath.

Jon kneeled on the seat in front of me and wrapped both arms around my waist. He laid his head against my chest, and I pulled him close, running my fingers through his wavy hair.

"I can hear your heartbeat," he whispered. "It's like a bass drum."

I bent down and pulled his face to mine. I kissed him gently on the forehead. He smiled and started undoing my belt, slowly pulling open the buttons on my jeans one at a time.

"Monica was wrong."

"About what?" I whispered. I was shaking all over as Jon slid my jeans down.

"I got the nicest flowers in the whole cast. Tulips are my favorite."

"Oh yeah?" I could barely speak. I kept my eyes glued to Jon's as he ran his hand down the front of my underwear.

"You know what's better than roses on your piano?" he whispered.

"What?" I choked.

He smirked as he pulled down my boxers. "Two lips on your organ."

I started to laugh, but Jon turned my laughter into a gasp. I saw stars. I'm not sure if they were actual stars, or just ones in my head, because my body felt so amazing. I'm not sure what I saw or exactly how Jon did what he did. I just know that he was really good at it. There were definitely no mishaps that involved teeth, and by the time he dropped me off here a few minutes ago, neither one of us had blue balls.

Sunday, September 30

Pastor Colbert's sermon today is called "God Hates Sin."

He's talking about how much God loves sinners but hates the sins they do. I feel like he's talking directly to me, like somehow he saw me and Jon last night. It's weird. I've never really thought about God having a problem with me—or anything that I do, really. I've always been way more afraid of people. Maybe it's because God is this sort of abstract concept—this big presence up in the sky someplace who supposedly sees and hears everything, but what does he actually do about it?

What Brent said to Tyler last night about rethinking who God was happy with—that sorta stuck in my head. How do we really know who God is "happy" with? Pastor Colbert seems to be the one who is most upset to me. He's all red in the face again. He just spouted out this long list of the people who make God mad: atheists, people who have abortions or vote for abortion or support abortion, homosexuals. . . . The list went on from there, but that's when I stopped listening.

I keep replaying what happened last night in Jon's Jeep, and I know I'm on Pastor Colbert's list now. I'm one of the people who makes God mad. It makes me feel terrible about liking Jon so much. How can it make God mad that we're into each other? How is what we're doing hurting anybody else? Or God, for that matter?

If it makes God so freaking mad, why does it feel so good?

Later . . .

We all drove to church together this morning, and on the way home in the car, Tracy asked Mom about Monica's uncle and whether or not he was one of the people God was angry about. I almost opened the door of the car and threw myself into the road. I did not want to be there for this conversation.

Dad was driving and said, "Hell yes, he is."

Mom put her hand on Dad's arm and said, "Boyd, honey. Please." She twisted around in the front seat to face Tracy. "Sweetheart, God is only upset about the actual sin. He's not upset that people feel that way."

"Oh, c'mon," Dad said. "What red-blooded American running back just 'feels that way'? He chose to be that way. Nothing else to it."

I actually got dizzy when he said this. Did I *choose* to feel this way about Jon? I mean, my dick still works when I'm with Monica, but it sure doesn't make me see stars. Why do things seem so much more exciting when I'm with Jon?

"Boyd, stop it." Mom's tone shut Dad up in a hurry. "Tracy, honey, being tempted with homosexual feelings for another person is just like being tempted to steal or lie or cheat or gossip. It's not actually a sin unless you act on it."

"But I saw this TV show where they said it wasn't a choice." Tracy was frowning, staring out the window—really giving this some thought.

"Probably because homos wrote that show," Dad said. "That's what they want you to think."

Mom sighed. "Tracy, the Bible says that it's wrong."

"Does it?" she asked. "I mean, I was reading this thing online that showed the place in the Old Testament where it said that it was an abomination or whatever, but then they showed this list of the other things God says are an abomination and we do lots of those all the time. I mean, you're not supposed to touch the skin of a dead pig either, but we all feel fine about football."

I laughed really loudly when she said this. My little sis can be a total pain in the ass sometimes, but she's really smart. Mom shot me a look from the front seat.

"Tracy, God tells us to hate the things that he hates. End of story."

Dad pulled into the driveway, and I was out of the car almost before it stopped moving, running into the house—like I could outrun what Mom had just said. *God tells us to hate the things that he hates.*

So my mom will *hate* me if she finds out I'm a homo?

I was just looking up those sites Tracy was on, and it seems like there's just as many people in the world who believe the opposite of Mom and Dad. Why couldn't I have been born to some of *those* people? I feel so pissed off that I will never be able to tell my parents the truth about who I am. They think I make God angry. I hate that they think this. I hate them for thinking it. Why would you decide to worship an angry God anyway?

Suddenly I've got tears streaming down my face while I write.

What the hell is wrong with me? Why am I so upset? I hate myself for feeling this way—for feeling any of this.

That's the saddest part of all, I guess. If being gay is a problem, *I'm* the problem.

Sunday, November 4

I know I haven't written in over a month. Well, I have written, but just not in this journal. I realized after the whole incident-in-the-back-of-the-Jeep-with-Jon entry that I had to stop carrying this thing around with me in my backpack like an idiot. All it would take is one wrong move, and what's in this notebook could end up all over the Internet.

I was just reading over my last entry, and after that day in church, I almost burned this journal. I took it outside with me that afternoon and tossed it on the charcoal grill out behind the garage, but something wouldn't let me throw the match. There's too much of me in these pages. Too much I want to remember. So I took the journal back upstairs and buried it in between my mattress and box spring—far enough into the middle of the bed that Mom won't find it when she's changing my sheets.

Then I started writing in a new notebook for English class the next morning. That one doesn't have any of the gay stuff in it. I try not to even talk about Jon in it. It's totally lame, too. I feel like I'm writing fiction about somebody else's life. It's full of dates with Monica and making out with her and how hot it is. It has tons of stuff about Tyler: his progress with his knee, how he's getting off his crutches soon, how he's excited about getting back in shape. I can tell he's pissed about the season we're having without him. We're still undefeated, and next week we start the playoffs.

I've been writing in that notebook about all the college football stuff. The week after I committed at USC, ESPN actually showed up at our game and shot some footage. They did interviews with me, and I've been on a bunch of sports talk shows on TV and the radio.

Jon has been giving me a hard time about all the publicity, mainly because he knows how much it bugs Tyler that it's happening. He has gradually won Tyler over because Tyler loves it when Jon calls me a "media darling" and tells me I need to borrow some of Monica's mascara the next time I go on camera.

Of course, I just smile when Tyler laughs like a hyena at Jon's jokes, because I know that Jon is purposefully bagging on me to throw Tyler off our scent. Jon and I have found an easy rhythm. We see each other mainly after our big group dates with Amy and Monica and Tyler and Erin. We'll all go hang out after the game on Friday nights, or go play mini golf, or to a movie or something on Saturday nights. Then, usually on Saturdays, Erin will take Tyler home because he's still in a brace that doesn't allow him to drive. Once they're gone, we'll make out with Monica and Amy for a little while and then drop them off, and then I have Jon all to myself for a little while before I go home.

Yeah, so I'm not writing about that in the other journal. At all. That's why I had to pull this one out again. Jon and I just got back from the big hunting trip. I got off a few shots, but neither one of them were clean. Dad and Randall mainly drank the whole time. They'd have had a lot more luck if they hadn't been so freaking drunk and loud the whole time, but I didn't mind. It was lucky as hell that they were loud on several occasions because otherwise Jon and I wouldn't have heard them. Randall almost caught me with my pants around my ankles in the middle of the forest yesterday evening while Jon was getting . . . well . . . "adventurous," as he likes to call it. I've never pulled up my pants so fast in my life. We laughed our asses off about it in the tent that night, but I was also scared shitless. If Randall had seen us messing around while he was holding a gun, I'm not sure both of us would still be alive.

Ironically, Jon, the only one who doesn't hunt with a gun, wound up being the star of the show. Right before we left to come home this morning, he took his bow up into the stand one more time and bagged a freaking buck. Dad and Randall were both fit to be tied. They couldn't believe it and kept talking about how Jon was a "regular Robin Hood."

The buck is hanging up in the garage right now. Dad's

draining it tonight, and then he's gonna skin it and clean it
tomorrow night. Mom is less than thrilled about the deer
carcass hanging in the garage and all the bloody clothes she's
washing right now, but she's pleased about the prospect of
venison stew at Thanksgiving. She made Jon and me strip down
to our boxers in the mudroom and give her our clothes so she
could put them directly into the wash. Then she shooed us
upstairs to hit the showers.

I had to run because being that close to Jon in his underwear
always makes me noticeably excited, and that's a conversation I'm
not ready to have with anybody yet—much less my mother. In fact,
I don't intend to talk to her about that ever. I'm just going to get to
California. That's pretty much as far as the plan goes right now.

But that's enough.

I'll figure out the rest when I get there.

I'm getting ready to crawl into bed, and I keep feeling like
I forgot something. It hit me just a second ago that for the last
two nights I got to sleep next to Jon all night. The first night
when we got into the tent, we just lay awake and talked for a
long time, quietly so that my dad and Randall couldn't hear us
in their tents. I think we were both too scared to actually make
out that first night—afraid maybe my dad would hear us—but
that's the fun part of hanging out with Jon. I have such a good
time just talking to him that we don't have to be constantly

making out. It's like I have this awesome, sexy buddy who I never get tired of talking to.

After a while I started getting really sleepy and told Jon I was tired. He sat up and kissed me good night. Then scooted his sleeping bag over so that I could feel him behind me. He put his arm around me and pulled me close to him, and within a few minutes, I could tell he was asleep. It felt so good just to lie there next to him like that.

I wish I could do that every night.

Monday, November 5

After classes today, Tyler walked with me to the locker room before he left for physical therapy. We passed Amy and Monica, who were selling tickets to homecoming next weekend. He reminded me that we have to get our tuxes.

"Wanna go with me and Jon tomorrow?" I asked.

He rolled his eyes. "Why does that kid have to come with us everywhere now?"

I got totally irritated. "He's my friend."

"Yeah, got it, man."

"What has he ever done to you, Tyler?" I tried to keep my voice calm, but I could tell I sounded annoyed.

"I'm just sick of hearing about how he's the best at everything. He's the star of the show. He's got the fastest two

208

hundred on the swim team. He's a great singer. He bagged a buck. Blah blah blah."

"It's not Jon's fault he's good at a bunch of stuff," I said. "You even think he's funny when he's bagging on me."

"I just miss hanging out when it was just you and me, man." Tyler actually sounded sincere when he said this.

I smiled at him. "Dude. Chill out. It's just a trip to the freaking mall. You don't have to throw him a parade."

"Fine," he said. "Whatever. When are we going?"

"Let's hit it after practice tomorrow night. I'll pick you up. Text me when you're home from physical therapy."

It still makes me nervous to hang out with Tyler and Jon at the same time. I don't know why. It used to be that I was afraid that Tyler would call Jon names and stuff. Now I think it's more that he'll figure out something's going on between me and Jon.

God, I hate this whole situation sometimes. It's just so complicated. It's bad enough trying to hide this from Monica and my mom and dad. I wish I had somebody I could talk to about this who would get it. There are these sites online that offer "support for gay teens." They all have hotlines to call, but what would I say if I called? I clicked onto a chat screen on one of the sites, and somebody came on and asked if they could help me. I just sat there staring at the curser blinking on the screen; then I closed the box.

I mean, what's my end game here? Play well at college? Then what? Hopefully get drafted into the NFL? I mean, even if that were a possibility, I'm not gonna be able to come out then. Sure, there are people coming out of the closet all over sports. But football? And then have it be all over the news? My dad would flip his shit. Mom would have a breakdown. How is somebody sitting at a computer on the other side of the country going to fix that? How are they going to be able to help me?

This is what happens when I let my head run with this idea. It just seems totally hopeless. But how long can I hide what's going on with me and Jon?

Tuesday, November 6

We actually had fun getting fitted for tuxedos. After practice, I picked up Tyler, and then we swung by to get Jon. He had called the place over by the mall to make sure they'd still be open after I got done with practice at six p.m.

When we got there, we looked around at the mannequins and at the selections they had hanging on the racks. I decided to go with basic black, single breasted with a white shirt. The shirt I picked has a full lay-down collar with French cuffs. My grandpa gave me some cuff links before he died that I've never really worn, so I decided I'd try them out.

Jon went with an ivory-colored dinner jacket with a shawl

collar and black tuxedo pants. I think he's going to go with a long skinny tie. He kept talking about Frank Sinatra and the Rat Pack as his inspiration.

I held Tyler's crutches for him, and he hopped into the dressing room to try on a few things. When he poked his head out of the door, he had this grin on his face, and I realized I hadn't seen him smile in a long time.

"You assholes ready for this?" he asked.

Without waiting for an answer, he swung the door open and took a couple of hops out into the area by the mirror, holding his leg in the brace out in front of him. He was wearing a powder-blue tuxedo that looked like it came straight from the seventies, with a giant ruffled shirt and a bow tie the size of my head. I almost fell down, I started laughing so hard. Jon silently walked over and held up his hand for a high five. Tyler laughed and smacked it.

"You win, man," said Jon. "That's the bomb."

"You think this is it?" Tyler asked.

"Dude . . ." I was wiping tears out of my eyes. "If you wear that, you are the biggest badass our school has ever seen."

Tyler looked at the lady who was running the place and said, "I'll take it."

He says he'll be off his crutches for the dance on Friday. Hopefully Erin won't kick him in the knee when he shows up that night.

Wednesday, November 7
Study Hall—Fifth Period

I am so pissed right now, I don't know what else to do except write about it. Thank God I threw this journal into my backpack this morning because I had it out last night and was running late to school this morning. So, instead of taking the time to hide it under the mattress again, I just tossed it in with my books. It's almost like I knew I'd need to write in it.

I'm not sure if I'm more mad at Tyler or at Jon. Tyler was just a total dick at lunch, but then what about Jon? How come he didn't give me the whole story? I mean, what is his deal?

Okay, I have to start at the beginning. I'm so angry, I can barely sit in this study hall. I feel like running until I freaking drop dead.

So, we're sitting at lunch today. Jon is telling Tyler and me how much the limo his dad is renting for us is going to set us back. Once we get the financial details worked out, we spring it on the girls: We're picking you up in a limo. Amy, Monica, and Erin are totally excited about it. Monica is practically in tears. She throws her arms around my neck and kisses me full on the lips right in the middle of the cafeteria.

"Was this your idea?"

I shake my head. "No. I was gonna toss you in the back of my truck."

She giggled and said, "Then who? Tyler?"

Tyler said, "Nope. This was all Jay."

We all sort of turned to look at him, and he had this weird look on his face. He was staring at Jon.

"You mean Jon?" Erin asked.

"Didn't used to be Jon, did it?" Tyler was still staring at Jon, who was sitting there sort of frozen, not looking at Tyler. His face had gone sort of pale.

"Jesus, Tyler. What are you talking about?" Monica could sense that Tyler was up to something. She has a strong no-bullshit meter.

"Dunno. Why don't you ask Jay here?"

Tyler had this smug look on his face that made me want to smack him. My stomach was instantly in knots. Whatever this was, I could tell it was going to involve Tyler being an ass. I remembered that night I told my dad we'd talk about USC later, and I took a deep breath.

"Tyler, what the hell?"

He turned to me. "Did a little digging on Facebook last night and clicked a few links. Found out our boy Jon Statley here used to go by Jay at his high school in Chicago. Big interview in the *Chicago Tribune* back when he was a sophomore." He turned to look at Jon, and his tone became mocking, like he was talking to a baby. "Turns out little Jay got picked on a lot at school."

I'd had it. I slammed a fist down on the table and made everybody's trays jump. Tyler held up both hands. He wore his little shit-eating grin. "Dude. Chill. I'm just reading what it says online. Isn't that right? *Jay?*"

Monica was pissed. "Tyler, you're such a moron. What does this have to do with anything?"

"Wanna tell her why you were being picked on in Chi-Town, buddy?" he asked Jon. "Or should I?"

Jon looked up at Monica and over at Amy, then glanced down the table at Tyler and Erin. He looked at everybody sitting there. Except me. Slowly, he pushed his tray back, slung the strap of his messenger bag over his shoulder, and stood up. He stared Tyler down for what seemed like a long time.

"Tell 'em whatever you want, tough guy. I'm out." Then he turned and slowly walked out of the cafeteria.

When he left, Monica whirled on Tyler. "You are such an asshole. What is the big deal? What was this all-important issue you just had to bring up?"

"Dude started a GSA in Chicago, Monica," Tyler said.

"A GSA?" Amy was confused.

Monica rolled her eyes. "A Gay-Straight Alliance."

"What's that?" asked Erin.

"It's a club where gay students and straight students meet up to be supportive," Monica said. "Jeez. Don't you watch TV?"

"They actually have those in high schools?" Amy frowned.

"Uh, yeah. Just not ours. *Yet*." Monica shot this at Tyler, who rolled his eyes.

"*Ever*, if I can help it," he said.

"It doesn't mean anything," I said. "Who cares if he started a Gay-Straight Alliance?"

"Doesn't *mean* anything? Dude!" Tyler was laughing. "Are you kidding? Before Jon transformed himself into a singing swim god and changed his name, he was the laughingstock of his high school. Dude is a total homo."

"No, he's *not*!" Amy was pissed now. "He's a really good kisser, and he's my date for homecoming. You're just an asshole, Tyler."

"Oh . . . okay. Sure. Great. *I'm* the asshole. Fine." Tyler crossed his arms and shook his head. "Actually, *I'm* the one who's telling you the *truth*. But sure. Side with the closet case who has you all dazzled."

I wanted to kick Tyler in the knee under the table, but I knew I couldn't. I couldn't stand up for Jon too forcefully, either. I couldn't do anything because I didn't have the whole story. I wasn't getting it from Tyler, that's for sure. I grabbed my tray and stood up.

"Where you going, champ?" Tyler asked it as a question, but I heard a challenge.

"To find Jon," I said calmly. "Jesus, Tyler. He's got a girlfriend," I said, nodding at Amy.

"Does he?" Tyler asked. "I mean, does he call you that?"

Amy sighed and stood up, grabbing her tray. "So he started a club, Tyler. Doesn't make him *gay*."

"Nah. Course not," said Tyler. "Just makes him a guy who wants to hang out with a bunch of gay guys."

"Or maybe," I said, "it just makes him *nice*."

Monica was on her feet too. "Not that you'd know anything about that, imbecile."

"Imba-what?" Tyler asked.

"You're the one into digging around online, Tyler. Look it up."

Amy and Monica and I tried to find Jon before the bell rang for this class, but his Jeep wasn't in the parking lot. I'm pretty sure he skipped out for the rest of the day. I tried to call him, but his phone went straight to voice mail and he hasn't answered a single text.

I could kill Tyler for bringing this up, but I want to see what Jon has to say for himself. I could tell from the look on his face that this really got to him. I wanted to reach over the table and grab his hand and tell him it would be okay.

Of course, at the same time, I also feel like shaking Jon and yelling, *What the* hell, *dude?* This is too close. It's too much. If Tyler could find that stuff online, anybody can find it. Once they do, how long before they start looking at me and wondering about whether I'm gay?

And am I actually gay? Shit. Why does this have to be so complicated? I don't even know how I feel inside right now, or what I want. My shoulders are so tense as I'm scribbling in this journal that I can feel the knots forming in my neck. It's like I'm hunched over this notebook, bracing for an impact, like at any moment the ceiling could collapse and the building and my whole life will come crashing down around me.

I have to talk to Jon.

Later . . .

I texted Jon from the parking lot after practice to tell him I was coming over. When his mom opened the door, she smiled, and I knew he hadn't told her what had happened at lunch.

"Jon told me you boys had a good time picking out tuxedos," she said.

"Yes, ma'am," I said. "Is he here?"

"Of course." She swung the door open for me and called up the stairs, "Jon, honey!"

Jon was already on his way down, pulling a hoodie over his head. He walked past without looking at me. "We're gonna study for our chemistry test, Mom. Back in a couple hours."

His mom smiled. "Have fun!" Jon was already in his Jeep, waiting for me. Mrs. Statley gave me a quick hug. "See you this weekend—in formal wear!"

I waved good-bye as I walked down the porch steps. I heard the door close behind me, and I took a deep breath, then climbed into the Jeep.

"What the hell?" I asked.

"Why did you come here?" Jon pulled out of the driveway.

"You disappeared, man. You haven't answered any of my texts or calls all day. What is going on?" Jon was headed down toward the park at the river and took a corner a little too fast. "Jesus, dude. Slow down."

He didn't speak again until we were parked not far from where we had gotten into the backseat together a month ago. Jon jumped out and slammed the door, then walked toward the picnic tables under some big elm trees. In the distance, I could see joggers and bikers and moms with strollers on the running path that crossed the bridge by the dam. I followed Jon to one of the stone tables. He sat on it with his feet on the bench, watching the last light fade behind the hills.

"Jon?"

When I said his name, he didn't turn around. Instead he crossed his arms on his knees and buried his face. I slid onto the table next to him and put a hand on his shoulder.

"Don't!" Jon shrugged me off and scooted away from me on the table. His face was red, and there were tears streaming down his cheeks.

When I saw that, something in me snapped—not in an angry way—but like a light switch coming on. I saw a look of frustration and fear in his eyes that I recognized. I knew these feelings, because I'd felt them, too.

I stayed where I was sitting on the table. It was almost dark now, and the breeze coming off the river was crisp and cool. The lights blinked on across the bridge. After a bit I decided to try again.

"I'm sorry about Tyler," I said.

Jon rubbed a sleeve across his face and gave a short, bitter laugh. "But . . ."

"But what?" I asked.

He took a deep breath and his head dropped back, his eyes closed. "But you're here to tell me you can't be seen with me anymore. That you can't hang out with the school fag."

Now I was angry. "Would you shut the hell up?"

He turned and looked at me. Even in the dark, his eyes were on fire. "Why should I? Isn't that why you came over?"

I just looked at him and shook my head. "No. No way."

"So . . . what then?"

"I came over to see if you were okay."

Jon's body relaxed a little. "No," he said quietly. "I'm not. I'm not okay. I can't believe this is happening all over again."

This time the sobs shook his whole body, and I didn't even

think about letting him stop me. I just walked over and climbed up on the picnic table behind him. I sat down with a leg on either side of him and wrapped my arms around him. Finally he leaned in to me and grabbed on to my hands and just cried until he couldn't cry anymore.

After a minute he was quiet, and we just sat there in the chill, staring at the lights on the bridge.

"Somebody's gonna see us sitting here like this," he whispered.

"Fuck 'em," I said.

He jumped up and spun around to face me. "Don't!" he said fiercely. "Don't *do* that."

"Do what?" I asked.

"Pretend."

"I'm not!"

"You are. You are pretending that you wouldn't flip your shit if Tyler walked up right this second and saw you sitting there with your arms and legs wrapped around me."

I looked away. He was right. I hated Tyler. And myself for caring.

"Why didn't you just tell me?" I asked.

"Tell you what?" he said.

"That you're gay?"

He looked at me like I'd grown antlers. "Are you insane?

'Oh, hi. I'm Jay the new kid from Chicago, and I'd like to inform the hottest guy in class on my first day of school that I'm a homo who wants to make out with you.'"

He collapsed back onto the bench of the table where I was still sitting. I swung around and sat next to him. "I get it," I said.

"Do you?" he asked. His voice was quiet, and his eyes were staring out at the river but seeing something far away. "Do you get what it's like to be picked on every single day of your life at school? Do you get what it's like to found a Gay-Straight Alliance as a sophomore so that you'll have someplace safe to go, and then you're the only one who shows up? Just me and the music teacher for two whole years."

"Is that what that article Tyler found was about?"

Jon nodded. "I was so proud of myself for standing up to the bullies. I thought I'd take back all those names they were calling me. 'Gay' can't be a put-down if I call myself that, right?" He shook his head. "Slapping a label on myself didn't make it any easier. It made it worse. Finally Dad went on a nationwide job hunt so that we could get out of Chicago. I untagged 543 pictures on Facebook and changed the name in my profile and moved seven hundred miles away so I could start over."

He stood up and took a few steps down toward the river, his

hands shoved in the front pocket of his hoodie. From where I was sitting at the table, he towered over me, his broad shoulders blocking the light from the bridge, casting a shadow twice as tall as he was across the dark ground.

I stood up and walked toward him slowly, quietly. It was like I was approaching a strong, scared, beautiful buck that would turn and disappear into the trees if I made a sound or moved too quickly. I thought about our nights together in the tent, how he'd tossed an arm across me and pulled me close. He was so strong on the outside. I hadn't realized how delicate he must be on the inside.

I stood next to him, peering up at the lights. Cautiously, I leaned in a little closer until my arm touched his. I felt him tense and then relax. His breath was still ragged from crying.

"You know what sucks the worst about it? I don't have a problem being gay. It's everybody else."

I reached down and took his hand. "I don't have a problem with it."

He gripped my hand and swung it up so I could see our fingers intertwined. "You don't have a problem with *me* taking a label. It's just not one *you* want."

"That a deal breaker?" I asked.

"No," he said. "I just don't know how to protect you from the fallout. I mean, if Tyler tells everybody . . . I feel like I'm radioactive. The 'gay' will somehow rub off on you. It's not fair.

You should be able to come out whenever you want. Or not at all. We should just be able to have . . . whatever this is without the . . ." His voice trailed off.

"Bullshit."

He smiled for the first time all evening. "I was gonna say 'pressure,' but, yeah. Bullshit is better."

"Tyler won't tell anybody."

"How do you know?" he asked.

"'Cause there's nothing to tell. I made him show me the article he was talking about online. It doesn't say anything about you being gay. The whole point of the article is about bullying, and they interview lots of kids."

"It's fairly obvious, don't you think? I mean, lots of kids got picked on. I was the only one who founded a GSA."

I shrugged. "We had it out with him," I said.

"You what?"

"Monica, Amy, and I tracked him down after study hall. Monica told him that if he spread any rumors about you, she'd tell Mrs. Harrison that Erin has been writing his reports in English."

"He's not scared of that."

"Like hell he isn't," I said. "He might be able to recover from a knee injury, but his scholarship won't survive flunking English. Harrison has a zero-cheating policy, and she's done it before."

223

"I can't just act like nothing ever happened. He *knows*."

"Jon, Tyler isn't that smart. By the time we have a drink in the limo on Saturday, he'll forget all about it."

"There's no way I'm going to homecoming with you guys."

"You have to, man." I spun him around and put both hands on his shoulders. "You change anything now, you run and hide? It's game over. Tyler will know he's won."

Jon considered this for a moment, then nodded.

I took his hand again and we walked back toward his Jeep in the parking lot. "Hottest guy in school, huh?"

"Shit," he said. "So much for playing it cool."

We got into the Jeep, and before he could put it in gear, I slipped an arm around his neck and pulled him over for a kiss. His lips were salty from tears, and as he leaned in to me, I felt my stomach drop back into place. I didn't realize how close I'd come to losing this thing that we have between us until that very moment, and the kiss made my knees weak with relief.

"This thing between us—whatever it is—I can't . . . I'm not ready to . . . put a label on it," I whispered.

"I know," he said.

"But I don't want it to stop."

He nodded and smiled, putting his hand against my cheek. "Me neither," he said.

Then we drove back to his place without another word.

Thursday, November 8

I was right about Tyler. He was quiet today at lunch, but he didn't bring up the article again. Jon was nervous about joining us for lunch, but Tracker and Sears grabbed him in the hallway and were making sure he'd have a flask of bourbon at the dance.

Tyler dropped one of his crutches when he was getting up from the table, and Jon reached down to grab it and hand it to him. There was this moment when everybody froze as Tyler turned around to take it from him.

"Thanks, man." Tyler didn't smile, but at least he wasn't a dick.

"Sure thing," said Jon.

And then the unthinkable happened. Tyler put the crutch under his arm, but he didn't turn to leave.

"Hey, Jon," he said.

"Yeah?"

"Sorry about yesterday. I was just giving you a hard time."

"No sweat," said Jon. He smiled at Tyler, and it was the kind of smile that made me realize why I liked him so much. It isn't just the broad shoulders, or the handsome face, or the abs, or the eyes. It was a smile that didn't hold anything back, a smile that said, I will try again—even when I have no good reason to.

It was the first time I understood what true courage looks like. It's not throwing a punch, or making a tackle, or fighting back. It's forgiving somebody who treats you like crap and giving them a chance to make it better.

Saturday, November 10

Jon had a swim meet today and Tyler still can't drive, so I was elected to go pick up the tuxes. We won again last night. That reporter Roger Jackson called me and wants to meet up tomorrow afternoon to do a feature interview with me for the front of the sports section when playoffs start next weekend. I think Dad almost had a stroke, he was so excited. Best part of this weekend is that Monday is Veterans Day, so we have school off. Have to go grab those tuxes now so we can get this party started. Tyler and Jon are both coming here to get ready. Gotta hustle so I can get in the shower before they get here.

Later . . .

Tyler's in the shower right now.

He was already here when I got back with the tuxes. Mom let him in, and he went up to my room and was on my computer playing this online game we used to play together all the time. I said "hi" and jumped in the shower right away. When I came back into my room, I have to admit, it was kind of cool to see him sitting there in his bright red Razorbacks hoodie, just hanging out—like it used to be. Makes me miss the days before he hurt his leg and things got complicated between us. Oh! The other surprise is that Tyler's off his crutches finally. Erin doesn't know, and she's gonna flip 'cause she was bummed that they wouldn't really be able to dance much.

I think Jon pulled up. I just got nervous. I hope he thinks I look okay in this monkey suit.

Sunday, November 11

Last night was incredible. Jon is still asleep in my bed, and I'm lying here writing about it.

I kind of can't believe it, but I was able to beg off from going to church this morning. Dad never cares, but Mom can be kind of a stickler about it. She was so happy to see all of us dressed up and having a good time last night. She took one billion pictures and told me on the way out the door that she wouldn't wait up for us and that I didn't have to get up early and go to church. I'm sure Amy wasn't so lucky. She's probably sitting in the choir loft right now with a hangover.

The limo Jon got was off the hook. Tyler threw his arm around Jon's neck and gave him a fist bump when he saw it. The two of them were thick as thieves last night, and it made me feel a lot better about the whole situation. Tyler's in a way better mood, and I think it has a lot do with getting off the crutches.

He looked hilarious in that powder-blue tuxedo, but also it was sort of cool in a retro way. Jon looked like a movie star. So tall and elegant in that white jacket with a black bow tie that really tied. He insisted that I get one, too, and he even tied it for me in the mirror. It totally turned me on. He was standing behind me with his arms around my shoulders, tying this bow tie, and my mom came into the room and took a picture of it.

That was the beginning of the picture taking. I swear we were the most photographed guys in the entire history of homecoming. After we finally got downstairs, Tyler insisted that he and I get one together, and it made me feel like our friendship is back to normal. He was clowning around in the ruffled shirt and then he insisted that Jon and I get a shot together. He took a bunch of us together in front of the limo. Then we piled in and went to pick up the girls.

On the way to Monica's, Jon broke out his flask and we spiked a few Cokes for the girls, then passed the flask around. He and Tyler were laughing and talking like old friends, and I feel really good about that. It's like they've reached a new understanding with each other. Or maybe Tyler just finally got the message that he can't go through life being a complete dick anymore.

The dance was a blast. Monica is a really good dancer, and after the bourbon in the limo, I was feeling pretty loose. I already knew that Jon was a good dancer because of seeing him in the musical, but at one point, he and Amy were doing this swing dance that was like something on one of those dance competition shows Tracy likes to watch. People just backed up for them and made space. He was whipping her around like a pro, and for a preacher's daughter, she sure knows how to use her hips.

Afterward the limo brought us all back to my house, and my mom had left snacks and drinks out for us before she went to bed. We went downstairs to the rec room and played pool and drank the rest of the bourbon Jon had. I snuck a few of Dad's beers out of his fridge in the garage, and then Tyler and Erin sort of disappeared for a little while out back on the deck. Monica pulled me upstairs into the living room, and Amy and Jon were on the couch downstairs.

Jon came upstairs after a little bit and reminded us that the limo had to drop the girls off by two a.m. so the driver could get back, or they'd charge us more. We rounded everybody up and piled in again, and there was just enough time for us to go through the drive-thru at Taco Bell. Tyler shouted our orders through the sunroof in the back and into the speaker.

After we dropped Amy and Monica off, Tyler and Erin rode back to my place with us, and for the first time in weeks, he drove Erin home instead of the other way around.

I'd already told Mom and Dad that Jon was spending the night at our place. My parents' room is on the main floor, and we were really quiet when we came home so we wouldn't wake them up. Tracy was at a slumber party with the girls on her gymnastics team, so Jon and I had the whole upstairs to ourselves. When we got to my room, I locked the door, kicked off my shoes, and started to take off my jacket, but Jon stopped me.

"Not so fast, mister."

I'd untied my bow tie and opened my top button after we left the school gym hours ago, but Jon did the rest. He started by pulling the bow tie off really slowly, and just that movement made me try to grab him and kiss him, but he pushed me back with an evil smirk. Then he slid my jacket off and tossed it over the chair by my desk. When he did that, I noticed it fell over something red that was already there.

"Oh . . ."

"What?" Jon asked.

"Tyler left his hoodie."

Jon leaned in and kissed me lightly on the lips. "Shut up about him, would ya?" He grinned and went to work on my shirt.

One by one he undid each of the buttons. He grabbed both of my wrists in turn and unhooked my cuff links. Then, slowly, he slid the shirt off my shoulders. His hands were cool and steady against my chest, and as he ran them over my shoulders and the white cotton fabric dropped away down my arms, I got goose bumps all over.

Once we were both down to our underwear, Jon pushed me backward onto the bed, and we made out for a long time. I finally rolled off of him and turned out the lights. When I turned around, he was already under the covers, and when I slid in next to him, he threw his legs over mine and rolled on top of me. I wrapped my arms around him and slid my hands down, down, down, feeling the curve of his back. I kept expecting to hit the waistband of his underwear, but I didn't. He was completely naked, and before long, we both were.

I'm blushing just remembering everything that happened afterward. We didn't have full-on sex. I've never done that before with a guy, and I'm sort of nervous about it. I'm especially not gonna try that in my own bedroom, just a few feet through the floor from where my parents are sleeping downstairs. We did plenty though—even some things I've never tried before. Stuff I didn't think I'd ever be able to do.

My brain quiets down somehow when it's just Jon and me in the dark. It's funny how when you feel this way about somebody, you get lost in their touch.

And what is "this way?" How do I feel about Jon? I almost wrote, "It's funny how when you *love* somebody . . ."

Do I love Jon? I don't know, but I've never felt this way about anybody before. I can't imagine not knowing him. I can't remember what my life was like before we met.

He just woke up and rolled over next to me. He threw his arm around my waist and asked, "What are you doing?" all sleepy with his hair messed up.

"Just writing," I said.

"Whatcha writing down?"

"The stuff I don't want to forget."

"Like what?" he asked.

"Like lying here in bed next to you."

Later . . .

Jon just left to go home. Mom and Dad are at church, and it was hard for me to let him out of bed. The good thing is that since we have school off tomorrow for Veterans Day, Monica and Amy planned a double date for us tonight, so I'll get to see him again. I'm actually spending the night at his place tonight. Right now I have to jump in the shower so I can go meet Roger Jackson to do this interview for the *Gazette*.

Later . . .

When I got back from the interview, Mom and Dad were back from church with Tracy and had made us a big Sunday-afternoon lunch. Her lasagna is my favorite. Dad wanted to know about the interview, and Mom and Tracy wanted to hear about homecoming last night. By the time lunch was over, I felt like I'd been interviewed for hours. Mom was showing Tracy the pictures she took on her phone of us in our tuxes last night. Tracy was talking about how handsome Jon is and how funny Tyler's tuxedo was.

"Oh—Tyler stopped by," Mom said. "He said he left his sweatshirt in your room."

I nodded and swallowed a bite of lasagna. "Cool. Did you get it for him?"

"He got it," she said. "I was up to my elbows in noodles when he came by, so I just sent him up to your room. He found it."

Suddenly I wasn't hungry anymore. I realized that I'd run out of the house to the interview and I couldn't remember what I had done with this journal. What if he'd read what was in here?

I finished eating and asked to be excused from the table, then practically ran up the stairs. This journal was right on the nightstand where I'd left it, under a bottle of water I'd been drinking before I left. My tux jacket that had been tossed on top of Tyler's hoodie last night was hanging on the back of the chair now.

I'm sure he just ran in here and grabbed it.

All that pasta made me sleepy. Jon and I were up really late last night, and then I woke up early this morning. I'm gonna take a nap and then head over to Jon's house so we can go pick up Monica and Amy together. So glad we don't have school tomorrow.

Later . . .

I am sitting in the chair by Jon's window. He calls it a "lounger," but there's some guy's name that goes with it. Eaves? Aimes? It's something like "Eaves lounger," but I don't think that's right. Anyway, it makes me smile when he says the name of this chair because he's very particular about it. Always says the name and then "lounger."

Jeez. I'm writing about this chair instead of what happened. Not because I don't want to write about what happened—I do. It's just I'm not exactly sure how. I mean, there's the simple way:

I just had sex with Jon.

But that doesn't explain it. I can write that sentence, and I stare at it, and I think about what my dad would think if he read that sentence, or my mom, or really anybody I know, actually. They'd totally freak out.

But I didn't just "have sex" with Jon. It was more than that. I mean, I've had sex plenty of times—with two girls. This was different from that. Something more happened between me and Jon tonight—more than what I've felt between me and the girls I've had sex with. I don't know how to explain it. We shared something so one of a kind that I can't completely wrap my head around it.

When we got back from our double date with the girls, Jon's parents were already in bed. Their room is on the other end of the house, so we didn't have to worry about waking them up. When we got back to Jon's room, we got onto his gigantic bed and started watching this show about an alien invasion that he's gotten me into. We didn't watch for long.

We were both propped up on pillows on his bed, and I had my arms around him. I kept leaning down and kissing his ear. Finally he pushed pause on the DVR and rolled over, pinning me down, and we started making out. Before long we were naked, and one thing just led to another. I'd thought about this moment a lot over the past few weeks, and every time I did I got crazy nervous about it. I mean, I know how sex between guys works, but it's one thing to know to do something in your head, and it's another thing to actually *do* that thing. I know *how* to throw a pass that Tracker can catch in the end zone. Actually *doing* that every time I need to is a different story.

Somehow, in the moment, I didn't feel nervous. When Jon whispered what he wanted in my ear, I looked into his eyes and whispered, "I've never done it before. Have you?"

He nodded. "Couple times."

I'd used a condom before when I had sex with girls. That much I knew. Jon walked me through everything else. He smiled a lot and even laughed. He made the newness of it fun and exciting. With girls before, it was all about me knowing what I was doing, even when I didn't. It always felt like I had to wear them down and get them to agree. With Jon, we were a team. We were in this together—we shared this moment that rocked my concept of what it meant to be a guy—the power and the passion and the tenderness. I wanted him in a way I'd never wanted anyone else.

After we were done, we just lay there, catching our breath.

"Holy crap." I sighed.

Jon smiled. "Fun, huh?"

"I don't think 'fun' really covers it."

We stayed there, a sweaty tangle in the sheets, staring at the glow of the lights from the bridge floating into his window. We talked about graduating next spring and college. We talked about plans for getting to California and what it would look like if we went together. Jon told me he was applying to film school at UCLA, and his dad had just told him he could apply to USC, too.

We started kissing again and ended up having round two. That's something that's way different with Jon. For the girls I've been with, once was plenty. Sometimes I think Jon and I could go at it for weeks.

Afterward we took a shower and then crawled into bed together. I wrapped my arms around him and held him until I heard his breathing level out, but I wasn't tired. I wanted to try to write all this down tonight. Sometimes I feel like I have these moments that threaten to disappear unless I get them down in this journal. I never want to forget tonight. Jon and I forged an alliance together. I can't tell anyone yet, but I know I'm headed out of this town. I'm going toward the Pacific, and I don't know what the future looks like exactly, but I know I want Jon to be there.

I wish I could tell everybody I know about what it feels like to just be myself. I wish I could explain in words how good it feels to be honest with another person about who I am. *This is who I am.* This is what it feels like to be loved. It drives away every fear. It makes everything seem possible.

Monday, November 12

I wish I were dead.

I wish that the whole fucking house would fall down on top of me and snap my skull off my spine. I want to be crushed between the ceiling and the floor. Better yet, I wish I had never even existed.

But I do exist.

And so do the tears that are falling onto the words I am writing. I don't remember when I've cried so much. Or hated so much. And all I can think to do is write it down. It's like the scratch of this pen against this journal is the only thing that's keeping me tethered to the planet.

The tears started this morning in Jon's driveway.

I woke up to Jon's phone blowing up on his nightstand. It kept buzzing and ringing and jumping around until finally it bounced off the nightstand and onto the floor.

I was still really sleepy, so I didn't really know what was happening. I just knew that it was bugging me. "Dude. Make that stop."

He pulled me in to him and kissed me on the back of the neck. "It's not as important as gettin' this." He rolled me over and kissed me softly on the lips. I kissed him back with more force.

It was our last secret kiss.

It was the last moment before we knew what the whole world already did.

Jon rolled over and grabbed his phone and held it up in front of his face.

"Shit." He jumped out of bed and had his laptop open on his desk faster than I'd ever seen anyone move.

I was still wiping sleep out of my eyes. "What?" I asked.

"Shit. Shit. Shit. SHIT!" His voice cracked as he yelled, and I jumped out of bed and wrapped an arm around his shoulder, bending down to peer at the screen. I thought maybe his grandma died.

It was worse.

On the screen was a video posted online. There were two

people in the shot, a little off center. One of them was unbuttoning the other's shirt, then pushing it down his arms. It was two guys.

It was us.

I jerked my arm away from Jon's shoulders like I'd been shot. "Did you take a *video* of us after homecoming? Delete that shit before somebody sees!"

"Are you crazy?" Jon jumped up and looked at me like I'd slapped him. "No, I didn't take a video of us. And it's too fucking late! Everybody has already seen this."

"What the hell are you talking about? How? How did this happen?"

He pointed at the screen. There were 3,207 views. There were 289 comments. The numbers were going up. I clicked forward on the video. We were down on the bed now, full-on kissing. That was me. On my bed. In my room. Jon was on top of me, kissing me. We were both in our boxers. I rolled toward the camera, and you could clearly see my face as Jon wrapped his arms around me from below and pulled me down on top of him again.

I jumped back from the computer. "Who posted this?" I yelled.

Jon pointed at the screen name at the top of the video: crutchFREE27.

"Tyler," I whispered, frozen as the whole thing washed over me—finding him in my room when I got back from picking up the tuxes, sitting at the computer. His red Razorback hoodie left draped over the chair that night. Mom sent him up to my room to get it when I was gone. I started feeling dizzy and grabbed the back of the chair by Jon's desk.

There was a knock on the door. "Is everything okay?" Jon's mom called his name. "Jon? Jon?"

I was gripping the back of the chair so hard, my knuckles were white. He laid his hand on top of mine. I stared at it, not understanding what was happening. I looked into his eyes—so blue and shining behind the tears. And then he smiled.

"Please," he whispered. "I can't do this without you. I love you."

The image of my dad and mom watching this video flashed through my head, then Roger Jackson and the interview in the *Gazette*, then the news vans that had been parked at every single game I'd had since I gave a verbal to USC. All of a sudden, I gagged.

I tore my hand off the chair and ran to the door of Jon's bathroom. I barely made it in time. As I was on my knees in front of the toilet, Jon opened the door for his mom.

"Honey, what's wrong?"

"It's happening all over again." He sobbed. Jon pointed at the computer. "Tyler. He posted . . . *that*."

He grabbed a bottle of water and a towel. He knelt down behind me in the bathroom. "It's going to be okay," he said.

All I could say was "No."

I pushed him away as I stood up, running into the bedroom in my boxers. I grabbed my clothes and got dressed as fast as I could. I could hardly breathe as I sat on the bed and pulled on my shoes. I could hear Jon talking to his mom, his mom pointing at the computer and then calling to me, but I couldn't make out what they were saying. I grabbed my backpack and crammed my stuff into it.

I was racing down the front porch steps, pulling my keys out of my pocket when I heard a voice call my name. I stopped and turned around.

Jon was standing on the front porch. He had yelled my name loudly enough that it must've broken through the haze. Then he softly said a single word, but I just shook my head and got into my truck. It was while I was pulling out that I realized I could barely see the road because I was crying. Something inside of me was breaking into tiny pieces. I sat at the top of Jon's driveway, ready to turn out onto the street, but not moving. I wiped the tears out of my eyes. I roared like we do in the locker room. I banged on the steering wheel until my fists were red. Nothing would cover up Jon's last word echoing in my ears:

"Please."

I roared again and pulled out of the driveway. I drove directly to Tyler's house and ran onto the porch, banging on the door with a fury that threatened to shatter the windows. His little brother answered. I shoved the door open and pushed him against the wall, knocking his glasses crooked.

"Where is the sonofabitch?"

He was frightened. "Who? Who?"

"Your fucking brother!" I screamed it at him. Full force. I saw tears form in his eyes. We were all just going to cry our eyes out today.

"Physical therapy," he stuttered. "He . . . he had to go to physical therapy."

I pushed him away and ran back down to my truck. My phone was in my bag, and I didn't dare turn it on. I didn't want to know if my parents had seen this bullshit yet. I was gasping for air as I sped toward home.

When I saw Dad's truck in the driveway, I knew they'd seen it. Dad never stays home on any holiday except Christmas and Thanksgiving. He wasn't here because it was Veterans Day. My stomach was in knots, and when I opened the door, I hit my hands and knees and barfed again. There was nothing left to throw up. I was empty. I wondered if I could stand up. I wondered if I could physically walk into the house. Something in me at that moment realized that all of this was over.

I had nothing left to lose. It was gone as soon as Tyler had clicked Upload.

My dad and mom were sitting at the dining room table with Dad's laptop. Tracy was sitting on the couch. When I stepped inside the front door, they all looked up at me. Mom was crying.

Dad stood up and pointed at me. "How could you?"

"Dad, I can explain—"

"Explain? You can explain this? No, I don't think you can. I'll be damned if any son of mine is gonna be a fag."

"Boyd, please! We discussed this." Mom jumped up and ran over to me, wrapping her arms around me. "Honey, we love you. We just need to pray. We need to pray that God will forgive you."

"Forgive me?" I asked. She pulled me toward the couch where Tracy was sitting. Had she seen this video too?

Mom knelt and tried to pull me down on my knees. "Boyd, come pray with us." I pulled my hand away. "Oh, honey, it's going to be okay. Pastor Colbert called this morning."

"Pastor Colbert saw it?"

"Oh yes, my little fruity football star. He called *us*. The *pastor* called us. His daughter woke up to a text message with the video on her phone." Dad pounded both fists against the dining room table, making the laptop bounce.

"Amy?" It dawned on me that this meant Monica had seen it. Monica. What was I going to tell her?

"Boyd!" Mom stood and grabbed both my cheeks in her hands. They were cold like ice against my skin. "Pastor Colbert said there is a good counselor we can take you to who can help you not be confused."

I stepped away. "I'm not . . . confused."

"Oh, so you *know* you're a homo? How can you kiss that little fag like that? I keep watching this video, and—"

"Stop it!" Tracy stood up and screamed at Dad. Her eyes were as red as her face from tears and frustration. "Just shut up! You're so mean. Jon is nice. And stop yelling at everyone." She ran out of the room. I followed her, slowly climbing the stairs.

"Don't think this is the end, buddy!" Dad yelled after me. "This is just the beginning. No fags allowed in this house. You think the coach at USC is gonna keep you on after this little stunt? You'll turn it around or I'll turn you around. I'll ship you off to military school for your last semester—"

There was a lot more, but I don't remember what it was. When I got into my room, I sat on the bed and saw everything like it was the first time. Has the area rug on the wood floor in my room always been tiny stripes of orange, red, blue, and green? How did it get there? I'd never noticed how many books there are on the shelves over my dresser. Did I read all those books? How did that happen?

How did any of this happen?

Tyler. Jon. That's how this happened. I turned on my phone. As I waited for it to power on, I pulled this journal out of my bag and tossed it onto the bed. I looked up and saw Tracy standing in the doorway.

"What's that?" she asked.

"A journal," I said.

"You write in it?"

I nodded.

"What do you write?"

I stared at her for a second. She waited. "Whatever I want," I said. "I write about who I really am."

Slowly, she walked over and sat down on the bed next to me. She reached over and slid her hand into mine. We sat there for what seemed like a long time. When the phone rang downstairs, I jumped a little. Tracy stood up and kissed my cheek, then walked into the hallway and stood at the top of the stairs. We could hear Mom's voice downstairs.

"Hello? . . . Oh yes . . . Mrs. Statley, no, I do not wish to discuss this with you. . . . No. No, I do not. . . . That is not my problem. Your son is sick. He has influenced our boy in his sin, and he needs to ask God for help and get his heart right with the Lord. . . . No, I will—No . . . You keep your boy away from my son."

The tears were streaming down my face again by the time she hung up the phone. I turned around and walked back into my room.

Sometimes the only thing left to do is cry.

And write it all down.

My phone keeps jumping and buzzing. There are almost twenty-seven text messages from a lot of random people. They're all about the video. Some of them are calling me a variety of names:

```
Fag
Fairy
Homo
Fudge packer
Cocksucker
Queer
Sissy
```

Several are from numbers I don't recognize congratulating me on "coming out." I have three voice mails from numbers I don't recognize.

I don't have a single text or call from Tyler. Or Monica.

I just got one from Jon:

```
Please. I can't do this without you. I
love you.
```

And Monica just pulled up in the driveway.

Later . . .

She was actually nice about it. I was half expecting her to slap me when I stepped out on the porch. Dad's truck was gone when I got outside. I'm sure he's at the Deadwood Lounge, drinking beers and trying to forget that he has a fag for a son. Monica saw me staring at the empty space where Dad usually parks his truck.

"I'll bet he wasn't happy about this at all," she said.

I sat down on the top porch stair. "Nope." She sat down next to me. We stared out at the trees for a while. It was quiet. Our neighborhood is strangely silent during the days. Big homes, huge trees, everybody at work. Green and ghostly.

"I think I sort of knew." When Monica spoke, I'd forgotten she was there somehow.

"Knew what?" I asked.

"That you were . . . with Jon."

"I'm not *with* Jon."

When I heard her sniff, I looked over at her and there were tears rolling down her cheeks. She quickly tried to wipe them away.

"I'm not crying because I'm upset with you," she said. "I mean, I wish you would have just told me, but I feel so bad for you and Jon. It's just . . . here . . . I mean . . . it's so . . . hard."

"There is no 'me and Jon.'" As I said it, I felt something twist inside of me, a sharp pain in my chest. My voice sounded like a stranger's, cold and hard around the edges.

Monica wiped her face again and tucked a strand of hair behind her ear. "Then that's gonna be even harder," she said. She stood up.

"Where are you going?" I asked.

She shrugged. "Home." She smiled at me, the smile that I'd loved so much on the dance floor at homecoming two nights ago.

Suddenly the tears were in my eyes again. "I'm sorry," I choked out. "I'm so sorry, Monica."

"You know, there was always some part of you that I knew I couldn't have," she said. "I'm disappointed about this—don't get me wrong—but it feels good to know that there wasn't something I was doing wrong."

I stood up and followed her over to her car. She opened the door, then turned around and gave me a big hug and reached up on her tiptoes to kiss me softly on the mouth. "Don't keep that part to yourself for too long," she said. "You won't be happy until you give it away."

After her taillights rounded the corner, I stood in the driveway for a long time and cried.

Tuesday, November 13
English—First Period

I cannot live like this. I had to walk through cameras and microphones this morning to even get into the building today.

Fucking Tyler was standing inside at our lockers, and when I walked up, he yelled, "Hey, dude. Heard you're switching sports from football to baseball. You catching or pitching these days?"

I almost slammed him up against the locker, but the whole reason I'm even at school today is so that I can play in the semifinals this weekend. If I don't play, I could lose my scholarship. And I will not let Tyler take that away from me.

When the alarm went off this morning, I woke up like somebody had fired a gun. For a second, before I remembered what was going on, I felt okay. Then it all fell on me like a ton of bricks. I rolled back over in bed and decided I just wouldn't go back to school today, but Dad threw open the door, like, two minutes later.

"Get your ass up," he barked. "You're not hiding out in your room. If you miss practice, Coach won't let you play this week."

I sat up and swung my legs down so my feet hit the floor.

"You'll be lucky if he lets you play at all. Now, I've been thinking about this. You need to tell everybody that it was just a joke. That you guys were just fooling around. Or maybe drunk. Whatever you think will make more sense . . ."

He was still talking when I closed the bathroom door and turned on the shower.

The principal made the news teams stay fifty feet away from the school entrance, but when they saw me park, they rushed over and swung the cameras and mics into my face. I had to battle my way through these guys in blazers and too much makeup until I got within fifty feet, and one of the school security guards told them to back off. They shouted questions at me all the way through the front doors.

After I successfully didn't pound Tyler into the floor at our lockers, I walked toward the English room, and Mrs. Harrison met me at the door. She pulled me over into the alcove by the stairs and gave me a big hug.

"This will be okay," she whispered.

I felt like I was going to throw up again. "No, it won't," I said quietly.

"You look at me." She took my face in her hands. "I have had you in class for four years. You have never backed down from a challenge yet. I'm not saying it won't be hard, but you can do it."

I nodded, but I don't feel her resolve. I feel numb. I can't believe this is my life.

Jon just walked in the door. He's five minutes late, and he looks like he hasn't slept at all. I'm sure he wasn't in the pool this morning. He just handed Mrs. Harrison his hall pass and sat down. I can feel him looking at me, and I can't look. My eyes are welling up again, and I can't

Later . . .

I'm at home now.

And I'm fucked.

When I was writing in English class and Jon walked in, Tyler
fake coughed "faggot," and the whole class burst out laughing.
Something inside me wouldn't let that go. I stood up and turned
around and grabbed Tyler by the shirt. I heard the fabric tear as I
picked him up and hurled him onto the floor. His right knee hit
the desk as I did, and he screamed like I'd stabbed him.

I wish I had. I wish I'd kicked him in the teeth and just kept
kicking him until he could never scream again.

I got sent to the principal's office. He suspended me for
fighting for the rest of the day and tomorrow. I can't play in the
playoffs this weekend.

Tyler is ruining my life. Where does this end? When does
it get better? How does it get better? This feels like the most
hopeless thing ever. I hate myself for ever even thinking about
my secret, much less writing it down in this stupid-ass journal.
How can I make all this stop?

I just want it to end, but I know that it won't.

Later . . .

Mom just had to pry Dad off of me. I think he just gave
me a black eye. We were watching the news to see what the

cameras got this morning. Dad was on his fourth beer since getting home.

Roger Jackson's profile of me is supposed to come out in the *Gazette* tomorrow, and Channel 7 had him on tonight. They played a clip from the video—the one where my face rolls toward the camera—and interviewed him about me. He told them that I'd be missing the first game of the playoffs this week. As the anchors were asking him all these questions about the future of "gays in high school athletics," they played another clip of the video with Jon pulling me in for a kiss. Dad yelled and stood up and threw his beer can at me. It hit me in the chest, and then he jumped on top of me and slapped me so hard, my nose started to bleed.

Tracy screamed and ran upstairs. My mom had to pull my dad's hair to get him off me for a second. I ran up here to my room.

I can't believe that they showed that clip on the news. I am so fucked. I can't stop crying, and I know why Dad is so upset. I deserve it. I can't stop myself. Even after all this, I just want to see Jon again. I must be sick. I must be totally screwed up. But the only thing that will make this better is seeing him again.

Jon just texted me back. He wants me to meet him by the walking bridge.

Later . . .

I just got back from seeing Jon. I'm so confused. I don't know what to do.

When Jon saw me, I looked awful. My nose was still bleeding and my eye was turning purple and really swollen from where Dad hit me. He took one look at me and started to cry.

"Oh my God, are you okay?"

I just shrugged.

"Did your dad do that to you?" he asked. "My parents said you can come stay at our place if you need to."

I started crying again when he said that. Just being around him made my heart race, and I was sick of it. I was sick of all this bullshit. This had been a mistake. I shouldn't have come. There was no way I could be *this*. Even if it is who I really am, I've covered it up for this long. I can get used to covering it up for the rest of my life. I decided I just needed to get away from Jon.

I turned around to leave.

"Hey! Where are you going?"

I stopped. "I can't do this," I said.

Jon came up to me and tried to kiss me. I pushed him away. I pushed him hard. He stumbled backward and almost fell.

"You're such a selfish dick." I had never heard him speak like that. He marched up to me and pushed me back. "You think you're the only one suffering here, you asshole? You're not. After you pulled that little stunt with our boy Tyler this morning, what do you think happened to me?"

He ripped off his jacket and pulled the neck of his sweater over and down on his shoulder. It was covered in deep purple blotches. "How many times do you think Tyler pushed me into the locker today? And how many times do you think he listened when Mrs. Harrison told him to stop?"

The tears were streaming down my chin, mixing with the blood still caked under my nose. I could taste the salt on my lips and ran the sleeve of my hoodie across my mouth.

"I went to the principal and told him I wanted to start a Gay-Straight Alliance," Jon said.

I walked over and took a seat at the picnic tables by the parking lot and stared out at the lights of the bridge.

"It won't make a difference," I said quietly.

"Maybe not to you."

The way he said those words stung like I'd been smacked in the face again, and I laid my head down on the stone table in front of me and let the tears take over. I felt Jon put his hand on my back slowly, tentatively. I remembered that day in the hallway when we stared at the cast list on the wall. I remembered how I'd felt that with Jon next to me, I'd never fall down.

"Please," Jon begged. "Come back to school and come out. Be the first out, gay, high school quarterback this place has ever seen. I don't want to do this without you. I love you."

I sat up and looked at him. He didn't understand. He'd never understand. This wasn't the way my life was supposed to go. Why couldn't I have what we had without having to be some big role model? Without having to tell the whole world about it? Why couldn't it just be him and me in private?

I shook my head slowly. "I'm not your boyfriend, Jon. I never was."

Jon flinched like he'd been stung by a wasp. Then he smiled sadly, wrapped both arms around me, and kissed me on the cheek. "Were you ever my friend?"

The pain in my chest shot through me like an arrow. I laid my head on his broad, bruised shoulder and cried. "I love you, Jon," I said. "I just don't know how to do this."

"I know," he said.

We sat like that for a long time. Finally he said, "I have to go. Will you be okay at your place tonight?"

I nodded. He kissed me good-bye, and I watched him get into his Jeep and drive away.

Wednesday, November 14

I'm back down by the river at that same picnic table. I've been working my ass off all morning. Dad woke me up before he left to meet his crew this morning at five a.m.

"Get up. You're not gonna lie around and write in that journal all day like some pansy," he spat. "I've got a whole lot of shit that needs doing around here."

I spent the morning raking leaves and cleaning gutters. I trimmed the hedges and hauled all the scrap lumber Dad wanted to get rid of from the garage to the curb, then swept out the whole garage. It was good to have projects to keep my mind off Jon and my dad and this whole damn mess.

I grabbed a bottle of Jack out of Dad's stash in the garage and brought it down here with me. It feels good to be buzzed, to turn off my brain—or at least try to. I can't really, though. I keep having the same thoughts over and over:

You're the one who started this. You're the only one who can make it stop.

I've been thinking about this all morning, and there's no good way that this ends. There's no out for me here. Even if USC still wants me to come and doesn't cancel my scholarship, everywhere I go, I'll be the punch line of the joke. The gay quarterback who got outed on the Internet. I don't think there's a way to ever put the gay rumors to rest. I hate that.

The thing I hate more is that they aren't rumors. I'm just a royal fuckup. Mom says that God made one man for one woman for life—and that anything else is an abomination. She says that it's Satan tempting me to do stuff with Jon. I tried to explain to her that it's not "unnatural" or "perverted"—at least it doesn't feel that way when we're doing it. It feels like the most natural thing ever. But she says that's just the devil tempting me and that we have to pray harder that I'll be delivered from this homosexual temptation. Last night she cried and told me that it would be easier to go to my funeral than to have me be gay.

That made me cry really hard, and I don't know how to make this better. All I know is what I keep hearing in my head:

You're the one who started this. You're the only one who can make it stop.

Shit. I have to get back up to the house. Dad's going to be home soon.

Later . . .

I don't know how to do this. I don't know how to be strong like Jon. I envy him. Maybe it's because he's been through this before.

I don't know what I'm going to do.

I don't know how it all fell apart so fast.

I walked back up to the house from the river today and was in the kitchen filling up Dad's bottle of Jack with a little water so he wouldn't know I drank it. As I put it back in the garage, I heard a car park out front. It was Brent, Monica's uncle.

He got out of his car as I stepped out onto the porch. He smiled and waved to me. "Hey, man. Nice shiner."

"What are you doing here?" I asked. I was scared my dad would come home and see Brent.

"Just thought I'd stop by. Monica is worried about you. Saw the story on the news last night." He shrugged. "Dunno, just thought you might wanna talk."

I shook my head. "What is there to talk about? There's nothing that makes this better."

"I know that it seems that way right now," he said. "But I promise you, this part is as bad as it gets."

"Yeah?" I said. "Well, it's pretty fucking bad, so I hope you're right about that."

As I said it, I heard Dad's truck pull into the driveway and squeal to a stop. He threw open his door and hollered, "Hey!"

Without even turning around, I knew I was screwed. "Looks like you were wrong, Brent. It just got worse. But thanks for stopping by."

"You don't have to do this alone, man." Brent reached out and handed me a card, but by that point, my dad was running up the stairs.

"You! You get the hell away from my son."

Brent held up both hands like he was walking away from a man with a loaded weapon. "Just trying to help," he said.

"Oh, you people are *always* trying to help, aren't you?" yelled Dad. "Help yourself to some high school quarterback ass? Is that what you thought, you fucking pervert? Get the hell out of here!"

He pushed me inside, and I saw Brent shake his head and raise his hand to his ear like a phone. He mouthed the words *Call me,* and then Dad slammed the door. The phone was ringing, and he ran to grab it.

"It's for you." He tossed the wireless receiver at me, and I put it to my ear.

"Hello?"

"Hey, buddy. It's Dave Joseph, USC."

My heart stood still. "Hi," I said.

"Heard you aren't suiting up for the playoffs this weekend."

My head was racing, I was trying to explain, but my tongue wasn't keeping up. I was stuttering and sweating, and finally he stopped me.

"Was that your dad who answered the phone?" he asked.

"Yes, sir."

"He still in the room?"

"Yes, sir."

"Okay then, I'm gonna ask you a few yes or no questions. I talked to your coach earlier today. He explained about the tussle in English class. That over this video?"

My stomach sank. "Yes, sir."

He paused for a second. My cheeks were bright red. I was

mortified. Of course he knew about the video. Everybody knew about it. They probably wanted to take away my scholarship because of it.

"I want you to listen to me." Dave's voice was low and intense. "You've got the best passing game in the country. I don't give a shit who your arm is wrapped around off the field as long as that arm is passing for us on the field."

I slumped down onto the arm of the couch. My knees were shaky. I couldn't believe my ears.

"No more fighting?"

"No, sir," I said.

"They're gonna give you all kinds of crap down there. I'm sure of it. You have to not throw a punch in the halls. Go throw a punch into a bag in the gym. Throw a ball. Go for a run. You hear me?"

"Yes, sir."

"I have to put your scholarship on a temporary hold due to a technicality in our program out here," he explained. "As soon as your suspension is lifted and you're back on the field next week, we're right as rain. I'll keep it outta the press. Got it?"

"Yes, sir . . . Thank you, sir."

"One more thing. Are you safe?"

I frowned and glanced at my dad, who was pounding a beer in the kitchen. "Uh . . . I, um—"

"Do you have someplace else you can go?"

I reached into my pocket and felt the outline of Brent's card in my pocket.

"Yes, sir."

"Get there. Now. Text me when you do. You understand me?"

"Yes, sir."

I stood there, stunned, holding the phone after we hung up. Dad reached out and took it from me.

"That USC?" he asked.

I nodded.

"And?"

"My scholarship is on hold because of—"

Dad threw the phone against the wall with such force that it exploded into tiny bits. A shower of plastic shards rained down onto the floor of the kitchen. I tried to explain. I tried to tell him it was just a technicality—that everything was probably going to be fine—but he kept yelling over me and pushing me. He grabbed a dining room chair and shoved it into the wall so hard, it cracked the Sheetrock.

"Boyd! What's going on?" Mom and Tracy had just walked in from the garage. They stood there, frozen in the doorway.

Dad looked at me for a long time; then very quietly, he said, "You have disgraced us all. Tomorrow you get out of my house."

Mom ran to me and said, "Don't you listen to him. He's not

serious." But I knew that he was even before Dad pulled her away from me by the arm and smacked her.

"I'm dead fucking serious," he growled at her. He turned on me and held out his hand. "Give me your keys."

"How am I supposed to leave if I don't have my truck?" I asked.

"Guess you shoulda thought about that before you decided to become a fucking fairy, huh?" he sneered. "Maybe one of your faggoty little friends can come pick you up."

I stood there, frozen in place, but my whole body was on fire. Everything I'd ever hated about my dad welled up inside of me. My hatred and sadness and hurt was a torrent that threatened to knock me down. I bit my lip. I would not cry.

Dad lunged at me, but he was already buzzed and I sidestepped him. He tripped on the corner of the couch and landed in a heap on the floor. I tossed my keys onto the coffee table. "Tomorrow!" he screamed at me. "You're out."

Mom and Tracy were crying. Dad struggled to his feet, and as I walked up the stairs to my room, I heard him crack open another beer. I didn't want to risk Dad hearing me on the phone, so I texted Brent:

Can you meet me at the bridge over the dam?

Then I texted Jon:

```
Not safe here. Can I still crash with you?
```

I threw as much as I could into a couple of duffel bags and then grabbed this journal. I wanted to write this all down before I left the house. I don't know what the rest of this night looks like.

Or the rest of my life.

I know this doesn't stop because I go to Jon's house. I know there isn't a "happily ever after" for my family. There's no big play. There's no Hail Mary pass that's going to pull this one out as the clock winds down.

I wish I could make all this stop. I wish I could make things go back to the way they were before Tyler posted that video. I wish I could make my dad love me no matter what. I wish I could make my mom stop crying. But I don't have the power to do any of that.

I only have the power to do one thing, and that's get out of here.

Jon and Brent both texted me back just now the same single word:

```
Yes.
```

I told Brent I'd see him there in ten minutes. It'll probably take me about that long to walk down there in the dark.

KATV Channel 7 DAYBREAK—Live Report Transcript
Thursday, November 15

Amanda Tarstley (in studio): We now have an update on a story that we've been following all week. The young high school quarterback who was recently outed in an online video has been hospitalized for injuries sustained last night at his home. KATV's Roger Jackson is standing by at Arkansas Children's Hospital with details. Roger, can you tell us what happened?

Jackson (on location): I'm here at Arkansas Children's Hospital where eighteen-year-old ███████████ was admitted last night. Sources tell us that he is listed in stable condition after authorities responded to a 911 call placed by his younger sister, ████████. Police were called to the ███████████ home last night around nine thirty p.m. When paramedics arrived, they found ███████████ unconscious from what appeared to be a blow to the head. Authorities have not yet released a statement or filed charges, but from what we understand, ████████ 's father, ███████████, has been taken into custody.

Tarstley: Is there any word on how this will affect his ability to play in the final games of the season or his scholarship opportunities?

Jackson: Amanda, as you recall, ████████████ had recently committed to a full-ride scholarship at USC for next year, and I had just completed an interview with him for the *Gazette* when a video surfaced last week of him kissing another young man. The video was made in secret and posted by a teammate. There has been some speculation among those close to the family that Mr. ████████ was not supportive of his son's sexual orientation. The details are still sketchy, but according to my sources, ████████████ was trying to leave the house when his father allegedly attacked him.

As to his future, I spoke with Dave Joseph, a recruiter from USC who had been in touch with Mrs. ████████. He tells us that ████████████ is stable and was mainly kept overnight for observation to rule out a concussion. There were no broken bones, only superficial lacerations. He maintains that USC is fully invested in ████████████ and that he has their full and unwavering support.

Tarstley: A sobering report, Roger. Thank you so much for keeping us posted on the situation. We know that those of you watching at home may have a friend or loved one struggling with these issues. Or perhaps you yourself are a young gay person who feels unsafe or needs someone to talk to. There are resources available.

Tuesday, December 25
Christmas Day

For a long time, I kept hearing people say that things would get better, but I didn't believe them.

That night I tried to leave the house last month, Tracy ran up to give me a hug. She had tears in her eyes, and just as she kissed me on the cheek, Dad grabbed her and pulled her away from me. I turned on him just as I saw him sort of toss Tracy into the wall, and I lunged for him. I saw him swinging at my head with his other hand. He was holding a beer bottle.

I don't remember anything else.

When I woke up, I was in the hospital. Jon's dad was standing over me. He was the attending physician in the emergency room that night. Mom was there and Tracy. I didn't know it at the time, but Brent and Monica and her mom were in the waiting room with Jon and his mom. My head felt like it had been run over by a tractor trailer, and they kept me pretty doped up on pain meds for a while. I had thirty-four stiches in my head and face where the beer bottle shattered, but the cuts are all healed now, and the scars on my cheek are getting lighter every day.

Dad got sentenced to ninety days in jail and a year of probation. He's doing his time now at county and then goes to a house for violent domestic abuse offenders after that. Dave

Johnson showed up at the hospital before I was even released. He stayed in town for two nights until I got settled back at home. After sitting out the first game of the playoffs that weekend because of my suspension, I played in the conference finals that next weekend. I passed for a personal and school record in that game. ESPN sent a camera crew, and when we won, the whole place exploded.

I wish I could say this whole thing has a happy ending. If it did, maybe I wouldn't be writing in this journal anymore. I don't know. I guess some things never get better. My mom is still crying a lot. Most days I'm pretty sure it's because my dad is in jail and this was not the life she saw for herself. Other days she gets really upset about me going to hang with Jon. I've been taking Tracy with me a lot, just to get her out of the house. Dad has called a couple times and keeps trying to apologize. He tried in court the day I went to testify with Tracy. I'm not sure how that part of this gets better.

Jon's mom invited us over for Christmas dinner, but my mom wouldn't come. She threw a fit when I told her I was going anyway. I can't handle the tears all the time anymore. I can't handle the sermons about how God is angry with me. Stuff like that? I don't think that ever really gets better. I wish I could let my mom and dad borrow my brain for, like, thirty seconds and just see what I see and feel what I feel. I think it would help them understand. Or maybe not. Maybe they just want to see the world a certain way.

There weren't many presents at my house this morning. Mom has been such a wreck that even getting a tree up was pretty last-minute. I brought Tracy over here to Jon's. I didn't want to leave her there with Mom. I tried to get Mom to come with us, but she told me that I was corrupting my sister and that if I kept going over to Jon's, Tracy would probably wind up being a lesbian—like being gay is a germ you can catch or something when somebody coughs on you. The sad thing is, I don't think Mom even knows what she's scared of anymore.

Monica and her mom and Brent came over to join us at Jon's for Christmas dinner, and then we all helped do the dishes, and everybody else went home. Jon's mom offered to let me and Tracy spend the night if we want to, and I called Mom and told her we were staying over. We'll be sleeping on the couches in the living room, though. Jon's parents are cool with us hanging—or dating? I dunno what we're really calling this. Whatever. They're cool with Jon and me being together, but Jon and I decided we wouldn't push it on sleeping in the same bed at this point. It's been sort of a rough few weeks on everybody.

Right now Jon and Tracy are watching a movie while I write. It's this old Holly Hunter movie called *Home for the Holidays*. Robert Downey Jr. is in it and he's hilarious. He plays the gay brother who comes home for Thanksgiving and has to deal with all the people in his family. Some of them love him for who he is (like Holly Hunter), and some of them don't. The cool thing is that he doesn't back down from being who he is—this funny, cool, kinda messed-up dude. He loves them without changing who he is or hiding at all.

I'm getting better at that. I'm sitting on the couch, and Jon's head is propped up against one leg and my notebook is balanced on the other. Tracy is cuddled up next to me under a blanket.

I'm not sure if my mom will have the guts to leave my dad. Or to get help. Or to finally go to a PFLAG meeting with Jon's mom. Maybe she'll always think I'm going to hell. Maybe she'll keep making her own hell here on earth with my dad knocking her around. I want to protect her. I want my dad to change. I want to keep Tracy safe. Because of what happened with Dad, she's got a court-appointed social worker who stops by the house once a week to keep an eye on things. I hope my mom will get out of the house before my dad gets out of jail. I hope she'll file for divorce. I don't want Tracy living with him if he's gonna be violent.

But all those things? I can't control a single one of them.

Jon showed me that I can control something: being honest. First with myself, then with the rest of the world. This weird thing happened when I did that: I didn't have anything to hide from anybody anymore. I had no idea how much time and energy that was taking. When you don't have anything to hide, you don't have to worry about other people telling your secrets.

I have one more semester before I head to California to start at USC, and I'm not going back home. It's easier because I'm eighteen and I can decide where I want to live. Mom isn't happy about it, but I don't care. I can't afford to get injured again. I'm staying at Jon's until school starts. His parents were fine with letting me move in, but Jon and I talked and it feels like a lot of pressure to actually live with his family. Brent talked with Monica's mom, and Ms. Nichols is letting me stay in their guest room starting next semester. At first I was worried that it might be weird living with my ex-girlfriend, but when I was still in the hospital, Monica came in to see me with Brent, and she grabbed my hand and told me that she didn't care who I was dating. She just wanted me to be okay. There's not really a playbook on how to stay friends with your girlfriend once you're dating a dude, but I think we're figuring it out okay.

Jon just got an early acceptance to UCLA. I don't know if we'll survive the rivalry—Bruins versus Trojans is major. All I know for sure is that I'm glad he showed up in first period this year. Sometimes you just need that one person who really sees you—who sees through all the plays you're making and all the fakes you're trying to throw. I realize now that I had a great passing game on the field and off. Jon was the guy who looked through all that and called me out.

The thing about being honest with myself is that it didn't change anybody else. Dad is worried about saving his business when he gets out next month. He'll go right back to drinking. Tyler is still obnoxious and bitter and pretty much a dick. But you know what I don't have to worry about anymore? Him finding out something about me that I don't want him to know—or worse yet, that I haven't admitted to myself.

This is who I am.

Jon surprised me when I got here earlier today. He nudged me and said, "Hey. Looks like there's a present left under the tree."

There was one tiny box and it had my name on it. I grabbed it and we ran up to his room, where I tore it open. Inside there was a thin silver chain with a mini silver dog tag on it. On the front it said, ROAR.

"How'd you know about the roar?" I asked him, grinning.

"I come to the games. I hear you out there in the huddle."

I snagged an arm around his waist and pulled him toward me. "You make me roar," I said. He rolled his eyes and laughed. I kissed him lightly on the lips. I tried to go for more, but his mom called up and asked if he could help her in the kitchen.

"Read the other side." He winked, then headed downstairs.

I flipped the tag over, and etched in tiny script were the words from that song Tracy liked—the one Jon had made me love.

You're the one I always wanted. . . .

It hit me, standing up in Jon's room by myself, staring at those words: I'm sorta like that song. I'm the same tune and the same lyrics, but I'm playing my song in a whole new way, and all of a sudden I don't care about being a hit, because I actually mean something.

I can feel the little dog tag on the necklace under my shirt, resting against my heart. I can feel Jon on one knee and Tracy against my arm and a thousand fears about what the coming days and weeks and months will bring.

But mostly, for the first time in my life, I feel like I don't have anything to hide.

Maybe that's how "it gets better"—not because other people change, but because I do.

RESOURCES

The Trevor Project
http://www.thetrevorproject.org/

The Trevor Lifeline: 1-866-488-7386
Trained counselors are here to support you 24-7. If you are a
young person who is in crisis, feeling suicidal, or in need of a
safe and judgment-free place to talk, call the Trevor Lifeline
now at 866-488-7386. It's free and confidential.

Trevor Space: http://www.trevorspace.org/
TrevorSpace is a social networking site for lesbian, gay,
bisexual, transgender, and questioning youth ages thirteen
through twenty-four, and their friends and allies.

GLSEN (Gay, Lesbian & Straight Education Network):
http://www.glsen.org
If you'd like to organize a Gay-Straight Alliance at your
high school, GLSEN can help you get started. Go to
GLSEN.org and click on "What We Do > Gay-Straight
Alliances.

She was a good girl,
living a good life. One night, one party,
changed everything.

Read her story in her own words,
in the diary she left behind.

She was an athlete

with a bright future. She only wanted
to lose a few pounds.

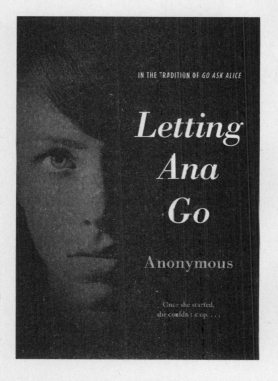

IN THE TRADITION OF *GO ASK ALICE*

*Letting
Ana
Go*

Anonymous

. . Once she started,
she couldn't stop. . . .

**Read her devastating journey in her own words,
in the diary she left behind.**

SiMONTEEN

Simon & Schuster's **Simon Teen**
e-newsletter delivers current updates on
the hottest titles, exciting sweepstakes, and
exclusive content from your favorite authors.

Visit **TEEN.SimonandSchuster.com** to
sign up, post your thoughts, and find out what
every avid reader is talking about!

Margaret K. McElderry Books

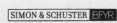

SIMON & SCHUSTER BFYR

SIMON
PULSE